Taking Out The Trash:
Garbage In...Garbage Out!

Antonia Ragozzino

BookLocker

Published by BookLocker.com, Inc., St. Petersburg, Florida.

Printed on acid-free paper.

BookLocker.com, Inc.
2018

First Edition

Dedication

To my amazing family and friends who I love more than anything in this world! If you feel in your heart that you are one of these people, then this book is dedicated to the love, friendship and support you have always given me throughout my life!

Preface

It is a typical school morning at the end of the third grade. I rise earlier than usual stretching and groaning. My sisters are always up earlier than me, so no one is in the bathroom. I scurry down the hall, quickly to get into the bathroom. This is a quest every morning with two older sisters! I splash water on my face and brush my teeth with my favorite Little Twin Stars toothbrush. My two sisters were already in the kitchen eating their toast and tea. As I get ready for school, my grandmother, Ella, who I am named after, would usually sneak into my room and make my bed. This is the shape of things to come as my grandmother continued this bed making ritual through my late teens. I am now horrible at making my bed because that talent, along with ironing, cooking, cleaning and taking out the trash was always done for me.

We lived in a small neighborhood in New Haven, Connecticut. My grandparents lived next door to us so it was completely normal for her to be over at any time of the day or night. My Italian world was ever so ordinary to me and my friends at our Catholic elementary school. We lived in a great big Italian community where most of my friends either lived with their grandparents or their grandparents lived next door. It was not uncommon to have an Aunt or Uncle down the street. Families congregated together for every meal or after every meal for *coffee an'*. I could never figure out what *coffee an'* was. As I got older I realized it meant coffee and pastry, cookies or any other kind of dessert. The *coffee 'an* my family referred to every night was just a simple, non-committal phrase for "let's get together again for the fifth time this week to talk more about nothing and eat again." The *'an* was the way out of committing to what exactly we were eating for dessert, but we knew it was something! My grandparents always hosted *coffee 'an* right after dinner. My Aunts and Uncles would walk or drive on over. I would get to play in the family room while the adults were talking. As soon as the lottery went on at 7:50pm, I had to go inside and get ready for bed.

Morning would come upon us again and my grandmother would come in at seven o'clock to help us all get ready for school. Every day I stepped out of the shower to find my Catholic school uniform pressed and ready to slip on for another boring day of school.

As I pulled up a chair to the kitchen table every day, my breakfast was being cooked by my mother and my brown bag lunch was prepared. Morning was not so bad. See, if I didn't feel like moving at a faster pace, my mother would let me miss the school bus and she would drive me to school. As I sat and ate my breakfast, my father would usually collect all of the trash from our bedrooms and bathrooms and tie it all up in the kitchen. My parents would exchange nonsense such as what is being served for dinner or which one was stopping at the bank. Then my father kissed my mother goodbye and left for work. These mornings were typical for our house. Everyone had their tasks and like a well-oiled machine, my mother and grandmother got me and my sisters off to school.

We attended our neighborhood elementary school, St. Bernadette's in New Haven, Connecticut. St. Bernadette's School holds eight classrooms of children, grade one through eight. I went through my Catholic schooling with the same students for eight years. My mother ran the hot lunch program. The program rotated each week from ziti, meatball subs to fried dough pizza. It was a very close-knit school and community. When the bell rang at three o'clock, we got on the bus to head home. Snacks were waiting when we got off the bus and my grandmother was waiting to collect our uniforms for a wash and iron. On this afternoon, my mother was frying chicken cutlets and my sisters, and I were doing our homework in front of the television.

I hear my father's car pull up in the driveway. I know dinner is close. My father always worked more than one job, but he always came home for dinner. We ate as a family, and then he cleaned the dishes, took out the trash and went back to work.

"Girls, dinner!!!" my mother shouts from the depths of her lungs. My sisters and I scrambled to the kitchen where dinner was served. Thank goodness it is Thursday because we always have chicken cutlets, mashed potatoes and salad. Chicken cutlets are my favorite meal. I sat right next to my father every night. I never talked much during dinner; my parents usually monopolized the conversation. My sisters and I just ate and listened to them.

I was the baby of the family. No one in my family ever had anything to talk to me about. I was hoping someone would have asked me about my first communion coming up. But I was usually not the source of the deepest conversation at the dinner table.

I learned later in life that I was always the last excused from the dinner table because my older sisters would sneak their food onto my plate, so it would appear as they finished their plates first. I was always stuck at the table last and then ordered to help clean up the dishes. Now I see how oblivious I was from way back then. I didn't even realize piles of extra food were snuck on my plate by my two older sisters.

My dad always stood and collected anything that needed to go out with the trash. He always took the trash to the basement and rolled out the trash cans faithfully on a Thursday night. I always knew taking out the trash was the man's job. My father, grandfather, uncles, and husband always took the trash out. It was automatic.

Somewhere along the path of my fun little childhood with my Italian family and respectful male role models, my life gradually changed significantly. Who would have thought one ex-husband and two big blue trash barrels would have such a significant impact on my life? Divorce crashed, burned and busted my bubble! The first day I had to roll my trash cans down the driveway after my husband left was the worst day I could remember back then. I just could not do it.

It was like a funeral procession but not because he was gone, just because I threw a fit that I had to take out the trash. Every trip reminded me that I was alone with no husband to take care of me and I was always being taken care of my whole life!

All these "man" things to be done around the house were not my job. After much time of soul searching and second husband searching, I realized not everything was ever going to be perfect, like my upbringing. I also was slapped with reality when I realized not all men were like the dads and husbands of when I was growing up.

We are in the twenty first century now and so much has changed. I am not a man hater. Actually, I am the biggest fan of love, I just have finally learned how to take out my own trash. I even brace myself every time when the man in front of me no longer holds the door. As soon as I became independent, I started to self -reflect, take my mental trash out and learn that I did not need to define myself by whether or not I had a man. I knew this revelation would have me embarking on a whole new journey in my thirties. I was smart, stable and full of good choices! Or so I thought?

Now decades later, my bags are packed for Killington, Vermont. I am all ready for my first winter on the slopes. So much has happened to me over the past few years. I am so young, and I just want to put my heartbreak behind me and start a new journey. I know my journey will never end with the same wonderful marriages I observed growing up, so I had to be happy with the hand I was dealt. My divorce, the endless search for a new man and my empty bank account just exhausted me. I was so ready to embrace life as a single adult, make new friends and shake men loose for the winter.

My friends and I are not your typical Killington, Vermont ski house renters. Renting a ski house seemed like a new exciting thing to do. We were tired of all the same, single things to do in New Haven, except for always enjoying the pizza. We wanted to get out of New Haven on the weekends. All of our friends were married and starting to get pregnant. As thirty something singles, there was nothing to do but interrupt our friend's happy homes on Friday or Saturday or go down to the city to strike up some fun. New Haven just kept serving up the same local bar events every weekend. If you are not a college student, there is not much to do for entertainment on the streets of Yale University. There was certainly no selection of men. The same men were out in the bars that were there before I was married! There was an occasional spotting of a guy who was newly divorced and back in the scene. Other than that, every weekend was basically a bad Groundhog Day. *Well enough,* I thought! My girls and I decided to learn how to snowboard, rented a ski house and rid ourselves of our New Haven trash. On that note, brace yourself for this series of "trash" tales as I chronicle more dates, men, mishaps and trips to the curb! If I keep taking the garbage in, it eventually must go out!

Chapter 1

I am sitting at the breakfast table with my new roommate, Gwen. She is moving into my beach house this weekend, permanently. I am so happy she decided to move in. I was on the fence about getting a roommate, as I did not want to go backwards, like a college kid when I was once a wife with a home. But Gwen is a good friend. She looks completely opposite of me with her blonde hair and Scottish features. But we are both laid back, get along great and truly have an honest, loyal friendship. I could not ask for a better person to live with. She is funny, easy going and the macaroni to my meatballs.

After a sip of my coffee, I look out the window to the end of the driveway and note that I took the trash out the night before. That was the best trip to the curb I ever had. On this journey to the curb last night, I had an epiphany about life, love and the fact that I had to start taking out my own trash in my head and in my heart. I realized that I am a great person who deserves the best. I am going to start thinking about what I will gain instead of what I have lost. What I have gained is a great job, wonderful friends and the means to enjoy my weekends with a new hobby and new people to meet.

So with that, off we go to Vermont! We rented the cutest little house right on the slopes. There are six bright young adults, both guys and girls, which we rallied up from Connecticut. I am responsible for the house which makes me happy because I feel it will ground me from being totally misbehaved and irresponsible. This was my big chance to take care of everyone and everything. After all, I never even got to make my own bed when I was young. Now I am in charge. I felt so alive on this perfect morning. We have twenty-two weekends and some days during the week to snowboard, ski, have fun, drink and experience this new escapade.

The car is packed with bedding, snowboard equipment, food and any supplies we would need for the whole season. My cousin, Liza, pulls up in her truck. I loaded all of our wears and goods we had been collecting for the house since we committed to the lease. I gave Gwen a big hug and hopped in Liza's truck. Off we went. I didn't know what to expect. It does not really snow that heavily in Connecticut and I am pretty much an urban girlie girl. I have not one athletic bone in my body, but I wanted to be cool and snowboard because that is what everyone does on the weekends. I brought awesome clothes for nighttime because I hear the nightlife and the clubs are the best part of the weekends. This is something no one in my tight little Italian group back home has ever done. We are so freakin cool right now! We pick up our other two roommates, Robyn and my other cousin, Jaime. We committed to getting up to Vermont in three hours to meet the guys in our house. Scott was my friend from work and George was one of Gwen's friends who wanted a share in our house. I am so glad these guys are truly just our friends because I do not want to be in a house with someone I am craving. I want to be free, have no complications and focus on ME this year.

I was gazing out the window at the gorgeous sight of green. The mountains and trees were so peaceful. Not like the smog of New Haven. And when you drive by Exit 2 off of I91 in downtown New Haven, it literally smells like garlic. We had a long ride and the girls were dishing about the guys they are talking too and I had nothing and no one to share with them. I definitely have someone I am interested in back home, but I think I just need to take the friend route this season and not get caught up in those terrible men who treated me like garbage!

As we drive, I can see Liza's car exterior temperature gauge fall lower and lower as we headed farther North. We could not believe how cold it was getting but I was still so excited. We had heard it got insanely cold in Killington. We know several people that live up in Killington which is where we got the idea of getting a ski house. Our friends gave us plenty of advice on how to handle ourselves on the mountain and in the bars. Our friends said, "Do not make spectacles of yourselves, the mountain gets very small when there are only twenty plus rentals." I do not know why my friend told us that, we would never make spectacles of ourselves?

Well here we are, pulling up our driveway in Liza's SUV. We all start fidgeting around in our seats and unbuckling in anticipation of the best winter of our lives. Jaime steps out first. I hear a big B-Boom BANG. She fell directly out of the car onto the ice. We all started laughing and we thought to ourselves that we were just not Killington material. We were a work in progress! Oh my God I am scared! These girls and I have been family or best friends for my entire life. Liza and Jaime are the same age and have been partners in crime since their first-grade adventures at a different Catholic elementary school, two towns over. These are the two peas in a pod who ran up their parent's room bill at the El San Juan for twelve days of jet skiing, virgin cocktails, lunches etc. thinking "just charge it to my room" meant it was free. They were ELEVEN! Now all grown up, beautiful, Italian, strong women, we have become like sisters and best friends. Our adult antics are not too far off from that trip in Puerto Rico over twenty years ago.

Robyn has been my friend for a very long time and bonded with Jaime and Liza from the second they met. Robyn, Jaime and I have long black Italian hair, and for some reason, Liza is a six-foot blonde. I'm not sure how she got those genes, but it was definitely not from my side of the family, as I am five feet four! Five minutes after I met Robyn at a Super

Bowl party, eight years ago, we realized our fathers bowled together and all of our sisters knew each other, and one thing led to another, now we are best friends.

When we stopped crying laughing over Jaime falling, instead of helping her up, we proceeded to unload the whole truck into the house. The men were not there yet so we snagged the best bedrooms. I immediately started cleaning and gathering up the trash from the boxes as we started to unpack all of the new stuff we got for the house. The ski house was three stories and very rustic with balconies and lofts. It was very Vermont. I wanted everything to be perfect. It was my name on the lease, so I wanted to make sure everything that could break was hidden and out of the way. We took a break from moving and unpacking and we sprawled out on the couches. Us girls made a pact and a few basic rules while on our break. No "drunk-dialing", texting any male, of any kind, at any time. "Drunk-dialing" was this new thing I was introduced to when I started going back out into the bar scene. For some reason, when you are drinking, your inhibitions go out with the trash and you just call guys that you like and completely embarrass yourself! And the last rule, no fooling around with other seasonal renters! See, if we hooked up with other renters, we would have to see them all winter. I jerked my two arms and two legs in the air and yelped "I'm not drunk dialing anybody!" I figured I had a new fresh beginning with people who did not know me. I was really looking forward to portraying myself as an independent smart young girl. Not the stupid Italian naive husband hunter that I used to be! Naturally, the girls did not believe me, but I was hell bent on proving them wrong. *Listen girls, I took my trash out along with the garbage of my past. I am not that girl anymore,* I thought. Just as I was about to utter those exact words out loud, I heard a large truck plow up the driveway. "The guys!" we screamed. Robyn, Jaime, Liza and I raced to the door and welcomed the men with clapping and jumping on our front porch. We had two male roommates, Scott and Greg. Scott was the nicest guy we ever met. I worked with him. He moved to Connecticut from Ohio. He was new to the area and asked if I had extra room in the ski house months back. Scott is an avid snowboarder. He is very quiet and very cool. He could go with the flow on whatever we all wanted to do all weekend. Scott too, was looking for a "good time" on the mountain and could not wait to see all the ski bunnies hopping along the trails. Greg was an old friend of Gwen's, we did not know much about him. He seemed harmless, free-spirited, kind of a wanderlust and we simply needed his rent share. In any event, the house was full, and we made our pacts, listed our responsibilities and thank goodness, the men were responsible for the trash. As it should be!

We were moving furniture and boxes, settling in our digs all day. "Don't you dare unhook those bunk beds, the landlord might get mad!", I told them. I was so nervous being in charge of this house. I hope this big responsibility does not cloud my fun, I just wanted the responsibility. I think it should be fine, we are all adult professionals in our thirties, not in college. Scott comes running up the stairs, "Ella we will put them back together at the end of the season will you relax and stop being the den mother. Fine, I will loosen up. Everything fell into place with our unpacking and we were done by six o'clock that evening. We were all gathered around the TV wondering what to do on our first night.

Robyn knew the most people on the mountain from back home, so she started making some calls. She comes back in the room and says "Everyone goes to The Barn the first night and the band starts at around ten o'clock." Great! We have plenty of time. We all started getting ready, showering, and making our own sandwiches and snacks for dinner. Our big dinner was planned for Saturdays before we went out. We packed fresh sauce, meatballs, garlic bread and salad. Tonight's dinner was something quick. Well, here goes it!

***

I was staring out our living room window, waiting to go out for our first night in Killington and I could not help thinking about this guy I really liked back home. I do not understand why it did not work. He liked all these tiny girls with long blonde hair but he always made me feel like I had a chance. My girlfriends thought he was a horse's ass. He used to always come up to us at the bar and moan before he spoke. "mmmmmmmmmmmmm Ella, how are you, mmmmmmmmmmm hugs girls, hugs". We would all have to hug him. I didn't find anything wrong with that. We got along really well. He just did not like me "in that way". I made such a fool of myself; I used to follow him all around New Haven. I got so upset one night because I was at the same bar he was at and he kept ignoring me. It was frustrating. I knew I hit rock bottom when I woke up the next morning to this text exchange:

> ME: *Are you going to continue to be rude?*
> HIM: *Huh?!*
> ME: *I walked by you three times.*
> HIM: *I'm at work? Where are you?*
> ME: *Bottega Lounge.*
> HIM: *Well I have a twin brother? Is it him?*

Oh my God! I was so embarrassed it WAS his twin brother. So not only was I stalking and blasting him for no reason because I was not even his girlfriend, but I was giving this poor strange boy dirty looks not knowing he was the TWIN! Oh well, I blew that one, but I still could not help thinking I wished he were here with us. He wanted to join the ski house, but he did not have the money. It was probably healthy, for me, that he did not go in on the house. I would have put all my irons in one fire, like I always do. I would not have allowed myself to meet anyone new. That is what I do; I get tunnel vision and do not explore all of my options. Funny how I get tunnel vision over people that do not even call me, text me or ask me out on a date!

The time for The Barn started approaching and everyone gathered back into the living room, where I was sitting. I turn away from the window and notice all the girls were in stiletto boots and tank tops. That is what we normally wear to the clubs. I said, "Do you think we will stick out like sore thumbs at The Barn? Do we know how people dress here?" Everyone concurred that it is not ten below zero inside, so everyone must dress like every other bar scene in the country. We figured we would just check our coats.

We all pile into Scott's truck and hit the main road for our debut at The Barn. We get out of the car and Jaime did not make it two feet without falling again. To see her skidding on her heels and falling all over the parking lot made me crack up. I literally almost wet my pants. I could not help but notice people staring at us oddly. Whatever! So, we walk in and immediately look down at the soot and hay on the floors. It was literally a barn. "Oh Fuck we look ridiculous", I squawked. We immediately gravitated to the bar. No sooner do I order a drink and my cell phone lights up with a new text. It is the twin! He wanted to know if he could take a ride up. Oh my God he wants to see me! I call over to Liza and show her the text; she gave me this scathing frown. "Have you lost your mind!? Absolutely not! No way! This is your first weekend; he has brought nothing to the table except a few drinks and collection of mmmmms! Don't you dare reply or I will take your phone and bury it in a snow drift!" I guess she was right. I mean he wanted to go in on the house with us and ended up backing out, so I was not going to put up with him wanting to use me to visit each weekend for free! So, I told Liza I would tell him he cannot drive up, there is no room. But, I never responded to him, instead I chose to do a shot of Jägermeister. Oh yum, definite drink of choice for the mountain. I was not paying attention to anything around me; I got buzzed and thought it would be a good idea to tell him to come up. I figured I would just do it and ask Liza for forgiveness later.

He called me, so I ran outside. It was literally twenty-four degrees below zero and I was in a friggin tank top! As my teeth are chattering I see Liza coming at me. *Oh Shit,* I thought. I looked at her with weepy eyes and told her he was already on his way, he asked if we needed anything so Liza barked "More toilet paper!", flipped her long blonde hair abruptly and walked back inside the bar. I was so excited, now I could relax and enjoy the night knowing my twin was on his way up to the house.

I scurry back into The Barn, teeth chattering. The guys were completely missing. When we went back inside, and we see Robyn and Jaime talking to two really nice guys. One of them had a college sweatshirt on from Connecticut. We sparked a conversation about the college and started exchanging names of people we might have known in common. They were such great guys. I was mingling, relaxed and kept buying our new Killington friends some shots. Mission accomplished, we are having fun and meeting new people.

Before I can say "Salute a cent'anno" pronounced as "saloot a chin don" which is an Italian toast meaning "health for 100 years", one more time, I whip out my phone. Rule number one, no drunk-texting was violated by me, the one who supposedly left her trash in Connecticut.

ME: *Where you?*

No reply. I put my phone away and continued bopping around the bar. At New Haven bars, everyone knows everyone literally since birth. There is no need to filter, have couth or behave in an impressive manor. This lends to me and my girlfriends acting very fresh when we are out because we do not care. Perhaps if we cared one iota about our behavior, we would get men. Now being over excited on our first night, we sort of forgot we were not in New Haven anymore. The four of us drag our two new friends with the college sweatshirts onto the dance floor and really start having fun. This was not club music, but somehow, we managed to fit in our same moves with this pop punk rock band all night.

Uh oh, I see Liza with drumsticks and a tambourine in her big bag. She stole them from the band. We sort of do that sometimes because we feel we have free reign in New Haven. We steal things from the bands, jump on the stage and pretty much run the show. So, we definitely forgot we were in Killington. The bouncer comes up to us and says, "Do you want to hand over those instruments in your bag". Liza flips her hair around and casually says "Oh no they're mine I brought them from home," and just continued dancing. The bouncer just walked away. So, there you have it, we were just completely fresh!

ME: *Where you at yo!*

No reply. Hmm whatever! I am dancing and bouncing around to the best band I ever heard. Killington was known for its amazing line up of really cool bands. I forgot how much I loved music. I did not even realize that because in my first decade of adulthood I was too busy trying to stay married and living like an old maid Italian to know such things about myself. I yelled to Liza "I have to go to the ladies room!" She nods and scurries over to one of the ladies rooms with me. I stand on my tippy toes and look over at the dance floor. Jaime and Robyn are dancing with the college sweatshirt guys. Shit, I forgot how I hate the line for the ladies room at bars. We are waiting patiently, and I keep looking at my phone. Liza was concerned; she did not agree with me having the twin come up but immediately supported me. I start rambling on about how I know he could not be here this soon because he had a three-hour drive but why wouldn't he text me from the car? Fine whatever. I need to stop being annoying and should not be harassing him while he is driving.

The bar is getting very hot, very crowded and very steamy. I guess hooking up in Killington is a big thing and as the end of the night approaches, everyone starts staking their claims on each other. I was actually glad the twin was coming up because it kept me on the straight and narrow. I just got a little intuition that he backed out of coming. *No, he would not just ignore me and not answer his texts,* I thought. I hate my intuition it is sick and always ninety-nine-point nine percent right. I felt as though a lot of time had passed, and I started to get a bit belligerent. I lost all of my friends at this point and was in a real foul mood. I lean up against the bar, order a beer and started shooting off the texts.

ME: *Really? Seriously? Helloooooooooo*

I go back into the bathroom and this annoying little girl is talking a mile a minute and acting stupid with a half shirt on and all sweaty. I looked at her with one eye almost shut from the Jägermeister. I just disgustedly lifted the air dryer facing up into her hair and her hair shot up like Marylin Monroe's dress, when the train passed under the sidewalk grate. As her girlfriend started to get in my face I ducked, dodged and ran.

Oops another New Haven Guido moment. I forgot where I was. Luckily the bars in Killington are so big with three floors and basements and different rooms. I escaped quickly. I found my housemates and we decided to start heading out.

The bars run shuttles, so no one has to drive which was awesome. We got in line for the shuttle and decided we would go get Scott's truck in the morning. I turn to my left and see a huge pile of pizza boxes. Oh, by the way, at night the bars make pizza! For real, this place could not get any better than PIZZA! I start asking for a pizza, the man behind the counter was ignoring me. Jaime starts taking over the situation. "Oh buddy, we need a pizza". The pizza guy turns around and says, "I am not serving you if you are going to be rude and not wait in line." Jaime yells "Hey listen buddy, I gotta house on this mountain and I'm going to be buyin a pie every night!" I swear the entire shuttle line turned to us and gave us these disgusted stares like we were mobsters invading the purity of the Killington slopes. We head home and sit around the table eating our pizza. We get ready for bed and just fall asleep independently either watching a movie or retiring to our bedrooms. I fell asleep on the couch.

After a twitch and a stir, I wake up in my living room. Oh boy what a night. I whisper, "Ok, we were good right, I think? We came together, left together, no harm done." I walk over to the kitchen and start brewing my ever so needed coffee. All of a sudden, I think of The Barn, the band, the boys and *Excuse me, where the hell is the twin with the toilet paper?* I thought. I race to my phone and I see two texts, NOT from him. The first one is my mother and the second is my friend from Killington that gave us the advice to not make spectacles of ourselves.

MY FRIEND: *Heard all the way back home that you guys were quite amusing last night.*

This is too small of a world. How did the news get all the way back to Connecticut by sunrise? Ok well take us or leave us, these people will have to deal for the rest of the season, so they better Fucking relax. We did not do anything wrong, except steal instruments and yell at the pizza guy.

Everyone started rising from their hungover selves and making their way into the living room. We started recapping the night. I really liked these friends we made with the college sweatshirts; I hope we run into them again. As I look out onto the mountain, the girls start honing in on me with questions about the twin. I said, "I texted him a few times and he never responded and never showed up". I tried to reason with them by making excuses, but the girls kept pointing out that it was rude, inconsiderate and bizarre to make me worry in case no answer meant he could have been in an accident. Liza did some investigating. She called her friend who bartends in the best club in New Haven. She asked her friend what people were out last night. It turns out the twin and his friends were at that same bar last night. He just chose to never show up and never let me know!

I was so disgusted, I got up, started cleaning the house, cleaning the dishes and gathering up the trash. It was piled sky high. I angrily stuffed all the trash in bags, tied them up and put them in the corner for Scott to take care of. Then I decided, Fuck it! I put on my snow boots and lugged the trash to the dumpster myself. I thought to myself, as I was trudging through the snow:

> *I can't believe I let this guy from home ruin my first night and keep me from really relaxing and being open to meeting new people. I waited and waited, didn't really go out of my way to be social because I*

had it in the back of my head that he was coming. I offered my ski house to him and his friends and they didn't even have the courtesy to tell me they changed their minds? Oh, and thanks, he was supposed to bring up more Fucking toilet paper! What if we really needed it?

I hurled the trash over my shoulder into the dumpster and went inside.

***

As I march back into the house, I slam the door and start rounding up the troops for our first day on the mountain. Some of my roommates are watching a movie, some are still sleeping. I go to my room and start pulling out all of the gorgeous snowboard clothes I bought back in Connecticut. I had a gorgeous snowboard ensemble that was black and yellow, so all of my housemates could spot me anywhere on the mountain, the ski lift or in a ditch, as I had never snowboarded before. Robyn and Greg were the snowboarders of the house. They were planning on teaching us the basics and then letting us fend for ourselves. I was a great skier back in high school and I was really excited to try snowboarding. I wanted to be well rounded in Killington. Not one of those girls that just drove up every Friday night to drink at the bars and be useless all day.

What I did not realize was how seriously difficult snowboarding was. Boarders have their own dictionary of terms. If you do not use them correctly, you sound like a loser. I was at the kitchen table listening and practicing my lingo. Instead of "snowboarding" you are supposed to say "ride". I was prepping to be the ultimate cool ass chick on the mountain. Problem is, speaking it and doing it are two very different things! When I bought my snowboard, I was fitted and tested with the perfect board, boots and bindings. It was determined that I ride "goofy" which means riding with my right foot in front instead of my left. Of course, I am "goofy" because why wouldn't I be? So, whenever anyone asked me how I ride, I would answer "goofy". It totally sounded like I knew what I was talking about.

My housemates and I are loading our boards in the cars and getting our seatbelts on. I looked out the window and could not believe how beautiful the snow looked on top of the trees on the mountains. It was so much nicer than Connecticut. Then I thought of Connecticut, where I have been, all of the trash I took out all these years and really wondered if I would ever truly be "ok." Liza turned around to the back seat where I was gazing out the window and asked if I was going to be a brat all day because of the twin. I said, "Absolutely not!! I'm over it." I wanted my girls to think I was strong, confident and basically not pathetic. Anyway, I saw three gorgeous guys at The Barn last night, so I am basically over the twin.

On the way to the mountain, Robyn was giving us the details about what to do, where to go and what the day was going to look like. We had to buy our lift tickets at the kiosk and put on our boots in the lodge. She prepped us for a rough day on the bunny slope, until four o'clock. Then we were to meet at the bar for what they call Après ski and suck down a few Bloody Marys. *I can do that,* I thought. What I was really thinking was, *can't I just sit in the warm lodge and wait for all of you?* Scott and Greg eagerly rode off away from us. They wanted no part of us, which was fine. Jaime and I had a rough time getting our gear on but we all ended up ready to go ride.

The bunny slope had this weird pull that you grabbed onto instead of a chair lift. I had no idea how to even balance on my board never mind glide up, to the top on this pulley disc thing. Robyn said do not sit on the frisbee looking disc thing, just use it to keep your balance, I had to put this contraption between my legs and have it pull me up the slope as if I was sideways water skiing. I was so scared. There was this gorgeous guy behind me in line. I kept giggling and looking at him over my shoulder cracking jokes. He really did not find me amusing. I guess I needed to take it more seriously. But honestly if he was on the bunny slope then he wasn't making out to well either!

I grab onto the pull which I guess was a called a 'Platter Lift'. Whatever! I got it under my legs. I ripped off into the clouds and I could not keep my balance. The disc/platter thing ripped out from between my legs and I was holding on for dear life. My right hand managed to stay grasped to the bar but my entire body, snowboard and dignity was sliding left. I looked like a stretched rubber doll almost completely horizontal, but I would not let go! All I could think of was that beautiful man behind me watching the whole thing in utter disgust.

Oh crap, how am I going to pull this off? I do not have one graceful or athletic bone in my body and you definitely need both to snowboard. I cannot quit, I must do this! I gather up all the strength I have and get to the top of the bunny slope. I was supposed to stay poised and straight. Instead, I looked like the water skier in the first scene of Jaws II! I was all over the snow. The journey was treacherous! I could not breathe, I had ice in my teeth and all I heard was Robyn, Liza, and Jaime cracking up and screaming at me. I gave them the finger and shimmied over to them on my board. I turned to look at the view atop the Killington slope and I was only a few hundred feet from the parking lot. The bunny slope was literally the size of my parent's lawn back home and I thought I rode that platter lift as far as the top of Mount Everest!

Well wouldn't you know the beautiful man behind me was a snowboard instructor? He came over to us and said "How are you ladies making out today, first time?" We made small talk with him and gave our history. I did not want him to know I was divorced and air out my business right away. I said, "Oh we are from Connecticut; we decided to do something different this year." He said, good for you, let me know if you need anything.

After a few hours of being able to snowboard to one side, the other, and learn how to turn on the damn thing, I was ready for a rest, but I didn't want anyone to know I needed a rest already! I think I did a pretty good job and the snowboard instructor kept helping me. I wonder if he likes me or thinks I am cute. Liza did great, Robyn is a natural, and Jaime and I were really ambitious to learn so we can get off that bunny slope. I took some major falls and wow, it is totally different from falling on skis, but we made it through our first Saturday!

When the sun starts to set after four o'clock pm on Killington Mountain, it gets pretty damn cold. I peeled off all of my ice coated clothing, gloves, neck warmer and hat and proceeded breathless to the bar. I don't really drink this early, but I have to keep up with the Jones's. We order a Bloody Mary, each, and spent a good ten minutes leaning outward from the bar, people watching. My mouth was so far open, I could not shut it. The men were outrageous, athletic, adorable and fit! I turned to the girls and said, "I am in adult Disney!" Jaime was touching her eyebrow, looking down saying "My eyes hurt with all these friggin men!" I was so happy, for the first time I felt like I could definitely get one of these men and I would be all set! My happiness and confidence were exploding!

We noticed another full room of beautiful people to the left of the bar we were gathered at in the front of the lodge. I heard music. I clunked over in my snowboard boots like a true regular and peered into this room of drunken skiers, snowboarders, a band and shot girls! I flagged all of the girls over to the entry way and nodded them into the fun. What I loved about this base lodge was that everyone looked a mess from being on the mountain all day. It was all part of the scene. I did not have to worry about looking good! How fantastic is this?

We found a table next to this gaggle of men who appeared to be on a ski trip. We sat, thank God, because my ass was killing me! A waitress came over and we ordered more drinks. The band was playing an acoustic version of "Me and Julio down by the Schoolyard, " by Paul Simon. The atmosphere was so upbeat. Everyone was enjoying themselves; Killington smiles were contagious at this base lodge Après ski. I whispered to the girls, "I feel like these guys are so cool, mature, nothing like the clowns back home, and HOT!"

The guy next to me turned his chair towards us and said, "So where are you ladies from?" We eagerly turned like moths to a flame at the table of gorgeous boys and told them we lived here in the winter but resided in Connecticut. There were six of them and they were from Boston on an annual ski trip. By the end of the Après ski, we got their names, what condo they were staying at and told them to meet us at Chatter. Chatter was another hot spot with bands and floors of Killington fun. Tonight would be our first time at Chatter.

Everyone started rounding up their gloves, hats, neck guards, equipment and headed for the parking lot. We were so excited about these Boston boys. I could not wait to see the one with the black hair and ice blue eyes. I forgot his name though. Oh well, I can figure it out by the end of the night. One day of snowboarding made me exhausted and starving. There was no way we could wait to shower, get ready and go out to dinner before Chatter so we decided to stop in the local market at the mountain. The market deli had hot delicious mac and cheese, chili and any other comfort food you can possibly imagine sinking your teeth in, after they had been chattering all day on the MINUS twenty-four-degree trails.

We all gathered at the front after we made our purchases and headed back to the car. This market was very deep into the parking lot with a huge hill for a driveway. Liza hadn't thought through the trip back up to the access road and did not know how to get her truck in four-wheel drive. We started up the hill and our wheel got caught. Now we looked like losers. Robyn was in the front yelling; how can we not get up the driveway with an SUV? We were all laughing and screaming and got so silly, we had to just stop and regroup. Liza had to call her father and ask him how to get the SUV into four-wheel drive. No sooner did two very cute guys come up to the truck and ask us if we needed some help. I was so embarrassed, I yelled, "Yes, we are from Connecticut." My friends turned to me and said, "Shut up, El, we look like tools right now as it is!" This was true, I mean Connecticut is New England, it is not like we were from Boca. I did sound like an ass!

Liza braced herself and got the truck in gear, as the guys were rocking the truck and trying to get it out of the spin it was stuck in. I turned around; the guys were covered in ice and mud. The truck suddenly took off. We were afraid to stop again, we just stuck our heads out all the windows waving and shouting "Bye, thanks so much!" The snowboard guy looked so angry at us for not stopping, or maybe even offering to buy them coffee or something. I don't know, we just took off and left them standing there with muddy icicles hanging off their noses and eyelashes. The whole parking lot was staring at us. Great! We nearly peed our pants the entire way home. Robyn was crying laughing. We could not get over the fact that we left those poor guys soaked, muddy, icy and freezing in the snow dust. I hope we NEVER see them again.

***

Scott and Greg came home from the mountain in a different car and we all got toasty warm by the fireplace in our living room. I was eager to get on with my night. I am so happy I put the twin behind me and tossed him out with the trash this morning. Scott and Greg were telling us everything they heard about Chatter, tonight's destination. It has two stages, three floors and is known as one of the greatest Killington nightspots. The bands that play at Chatter include solo acoustics at happy hour to famous bands that start at ten o'clock. Hundreds of vacationers, seasonal renters and locals gather every Saturday night for great drinks, music and fun! George met three snowboarders on the mountain that were meeting us, and we told the Boston boys to meet us at ten o'clock. I definitely had pick of the litter tonight. I think I am going to definitely like dating up here better than at home.

We get ready for the Saturday night festivities. I want us to take a cab because if I meet someone, I like to be in control of when I leave. There is nothing like talking to a tall drink of water then bam, your ride is flagging you "Let's go!" It is very annoying. The girls decide that Liza will drive and if we decide on leaving at different times we can take one of the shuttles. Music is beating and blaring, and we are getting carded to go inside. We decided to wear some low-key outfits tonight; nothing quite like our Italian garb from the night before. Jeans, cool t-shirts and Uggs seemed to be the ticket. We slowly travel down these long dark stairs into the main area of the bar. My heart is beating a mile a minute, as I round the corner I see a very surprising situation. There was no one there!

The four of us are walking around wondering where everyone can be on a Saturday night at the best bar on the mountain. We made friends with a bartender who explained to us that if you miss Happy Hour, no one usually arrives back until around ten o'clock. Um, ok it was EIGHT o'clock. Oh my God, we are losers again! I dragged everyone out of the house, lighting a fire under their asses because I had to get there to meet men and now we are standing in the back, staring at each other and drinking alone.

Whatever, I figured by the time the crowd started rolling in I would be all loosened up. We heard some live music upstairs. A band had started in the upstairs area for the earlier crowd. Thank goodness there was a few people in there. As I make it to the final stair, I see this really cute, artsy looking bartender who looked like he could be in a band, himself. He was ADORABLE! I scurry over to a vacant spot at the bar, twirl around and stake my claim on this area of the bar until further notice. The girls were just following along with their drinks and we all were really engaged in the band. This cover band was really great; they definitely had a good vibe. I kept watching the bartender to see if he was flirting or talking to a girl. I wanted to see what the situation was.

Besides keeping my eye on the bartender, I noticed there were very aggressive men at this place. There was a group of guys that were hammered. They must have been out since happy hour. Liza and Jaime went for a walk, I stayed back with Robyn. Robyn got us two barstools which was perfect. Robyn and I started talking about snowboarding; she was trying to give me pointers on what I did wrong for the day, besides making a jackass out of myself on the bunny slope. Before we could pause to sip our drinks, two very drunk guys from the hammered crowd approached us. "Hello Ladies!" We replied with a friendly hello. Robyn asked where they were from. They were from Lowell, Massachusetts. This one guy absolutely reeked of a cross between feet and brandy. He was still in his sweaty snowboard outfit and breathing all over me.

When he asked me what I did for a living, I told him I was a Surgeon and Robyn was a Paleontologist. Robyn looked at me and started laughing under her breath. I said in a low talk, "I'm not telling everyone what I do and where I live unless they have promise, just go with it." So Robyn went on with the lies talking about how this is our first vacation in Killington. We said we usually snowboard in Italy, but we took a break from foreign travel this winter. They really believed us. The one guy who was hovering and breathing over me comes out with this bizarre story. As he is slurring this ridiculous story about doing shots of Jameson every time he finished a trail his body is getting closer and closer to my barstool, legs and lap. I had my legs crossed on the barstool. I was leaning in to try to follow his story as it turned into when he is not snowboarding he likes to make red wine. I tuned him out and I was getting really annoyed. I am flattered to have guys talk to me, but they have to be the right guys. The wrong ones can take a hike. So, this man is telling me about wine and decides to rest "himself" on my leg. I started to squirm, and then I started to try not to laugh. When he was done with his story and asked us what hotel we were staying at and I said, "We are staying with friends and it would be fantastic if you can remove your cock and BALLS off of my leg!"

Robyn busted out laughing in her deep belly laugh and I turned to the bartender and ordered two shots. If I spent all night talking to these idiots I would never meet anyone else. I looked back at Robyn and she giggled "Cock and balls, OH MY GOD!" I said, "Robyn he hoisted his cock and balls on my leg to rest them as he was talking, get the Fuck away from me!" I am not used to getting this much attention, but it seemed like Killington was a big 'ole frozen meat market. I think everyone on the mountain got really horny after skiing, snowboarding, snow shoeing and snowmobiling all day. That is fine, but it is still my first weekend and I am feeling around the atmosphere, the people and the fun. Get AWAY from me!

Finally, the bar started to get really loud and really crowded. I had to hold my drink above my head just to walk around and it took forever to get up and down the stairs to the different floors. We finally all found each other again and planted ourselves right next to the side of the stage where another very cool band was playing. The girls were all together laughing, talking and drinking. We started to see familiar faces and I waved at every person I met from both days and nights here on the mountain. I was still learning names, but everyone was so friendly. "HEY COCK AND BALLS!" I even raised my drink to "cock and balls" as he stumbled by with one eye shut and he raised up both hands "HEY LADIES!" It was all so good it was actually surreal.

We were in no way ready to leave as it was not much past midnight but from across all the dark wood in the bar, I noticed the guys from Après Ski paying their cover charge at the door. The six gorgeous guys from Boston had arrived and they were mine! These dudes were more gorgeous than I had remembered from this afternoon at the base lodge. I wondered what it would be like to date someone from Boston. How cool would it be to find someone who lived in a very fun town and be able to go to Boston on the weekends? I was loving every minute of my wild imagination and just letting it go as they spotted us and walked right up to us near the stage.

Everyone was mingling, asking "Hey how is your night so far?", "Where did you eat dinner?" and just a lot of small talk. Wow, four girls, six guys and a lot of booze and music. I am in heaven right now. Just as I drag myself back to the floor from being on cloud nine, reality slaps me in the face with a row of shots lined up especially for us. We all pick one up at the same time and down it goes. I looked at Jaime and said, "Here we go again, night two!" Before I knew it, another row was lined up, this one was accompanied by individual slices of lemon and tons of bags of sugar. Scott and Greg were no dummies, they spotted us and joined in on the fun. We introduced them as our housemates to the Boston boys and everyone was just letting loose and having a ball. There definitely was one boy that I had my eye on, but I had no idea what his name was. I do forget people's names the split second I am introduced to them so that was going to be an issue this winter.

He had black gorgeous hair and blue eyes. That is about all I needed to know four shots in. We started to gather around the dance floor and went crazy to a popular song. Jumping, screaming, spilling drinks. All I recall from the song was "Pick it up pick it up pick it up". It was crazy on the dance floor, we were sweating and jumping around, and I needed a break. I walked with blue eyes to the bar and asked for a nice cold beer. I asked him if he wanted a drink on me because he and his friends were buying us shots all night. He leaned over and said, "I'll have a drink on you only if I can lick it off." Well, when you are drinking and doing shots all night that just sounds like the most romantic and amazing thing anyone could ever say to you! I leaned into his dreamy green eyes and started kissing him.

From that point on, we were inseparable and acting like we were in love. It was so fun. I was not really reading much into it. As our crowd filtered out from the dance floor and back to our spot at the bar, I could see the girls were paired off with the guys with two more to spare hanging with our Scott and Greg. Greg had some disgusting girl with him but who were we to mock? The Boston boys who were not lucky enough to scoop one of us up said "Hey let's go back to the condo we have food and everything." So, we all went with it, finished our beer and headed over to the coat check. Liza is whispering in my ear, standing behind me saying "I don't know if I want to go back to their condo. Who are they? We don't even know them." I said, "Liza everyone here is either on vacation or has a house, it is all fun up here, we are not in danger!" She was also giving the girl with Greg dirty looks, bending over into my ear "I don't want this ugly girl sleeping in my house." I turned around and said, "Liza you are drunk, who cares, let's just have fun at these guys house and we will all go home together, I promise!"

I was so excited, this guy seemed really cool and if I did not go to his condo, I was afraid I would never see him again. I ordered everyone in the car, I looked at Liza and said, "WE ARE GOING!" She just listened, scurried over to the car and got in. Jaime drove and off we went. The girls were good like that, they had my back, they knew I wanted to go. Jaime and Robyn were simply starving and we all just wanted more drinks. We followed both their cars back to the condo they had rented for the weekend. We walked into this really cool place and blue eyes went straight to the fireplace. Nice! Everyone was sort of walking around, waiting by the kitchen as the guys were passing out beers. Jaime ran right to the island in the kitchen and started opening up chips. There were bags and bags of chips, snacks, cookies, pretzels, etc. These guys were hooked up for the weekend!

I was walking around the condo like I simply owned it because I was with my new blue eyes. We were all having a really great time. We were all huddled around the coffee table, with the fire going. There was ton of drinking, kissing and random conversations going, like your typical after-hours party. I went into the kitchen and realized I was more starving than I thought. I eyeballed a large pot of tomato sauce on the stove with a fresh unwrapped loaf of Italian bread. Robyn, no sooner walked into the kitchen and caught me hovering over the pot. She said, "Oh no you did not start dipping into their Sunday sauce?" I mumbled something with a large hunk of bread in my mouth and ripped her a piece with a nice dunk into the pot.

Another moth to a flame situation, before you know it, the four of us girls were migrated over to the stove with the sauce, the bread, and I think Jaime was dipping pretzel rods too. Blue eyes came over and shrieked "Oh my God, what are you girls doing, that's our meal for tomorrow!" But he was half laughing, drunk and just started eating the sauce with us. Right after we licked half the pot clean, he insinuated that he had some pot. We were all in. We gathered again around the fire and everyone seemed to sit with the one they naturally were paired off with all night. Blue eye's friend presented us with the biggest bag of pot that I had ever seen in my life! I was sitting on the arm of the couch next to blue eyes with my feet on the coffee table. The pot started getting passed around. As we mellowed out a bit and were passing around a bowl, I started making conversation with my man.

I started out by asking him where exactly he lived in Boston. I would not have known where he was describing but I was just talking. It led into a deeper explanation of how long all these guys were friends and how they have been renting a condo in Killington for the weekend for ten years. I said that was so cool! I was all smiles until he said, "Yea but our girlfriends hate it, they get so mad and like want us to snap out of it and start saving money." My mouth, cheek and eye suddenly raised and became all crooked on my face. "Your girlfriends?!" I looked up and realized no one else was looking at us or could hear our conversation. He said "Well yea, we all have girlfriends, he's married" as he points to Jaime's guy. I immediately gained a keen sense of calmness. I took a sip of my beer and thought, why wouldn't they have girlfriends? It is a vacation spot, everyone up here is looking to have fun and I have only known this guy for two hours. What I was certain of was that I was pissed because I really thought maybe, just maybe, there would be decent single guys up here. Oh well, my bad!

As he is talking complete nonsense, I looked over at my right fuzzy Ugg planted on the edge of the coffee table. Next to it, was the enormous bag of pot. I bent over in front of him, so he could not see the left side of my body and I very sneakily took the bag of weed and stuffed it in my boot. No one noticed! Naturally, I turned him off and was not even listening to whatever babble he was spewing, and I eyed Robyn to go into the kitchen. She got up off the carpet and followed me into the kitchen. I said, "These jackasses all have girlfriends or wives and I just stole their pot!" Robyn just got into mission mode. We grabbed our coats and snuck out the front door while Liza and Jaime were playing a drinking game with the crew. We ran over to the car and I started it up.

We were laughing, hyperventilating, squealing and yelling, "We have to get Liza and Jaime!" I texted Liza.

ME: *Get your coats, they have girlfriends and are jackasses, I stole their pot!*

Robyn and I were laughing and looking out the back of the car to see when that door opened. We needed to make a run for it. A few minutes went by. I was just about to send another text when Robyn yells, "Here they come!" I back the car up next to the front stairs. Out comes Liza and Jaime with bags and bags of food in their hands! They jump in the back seat and I peel away. We had their pot, their food and Liza said they did not even know they had gone out the door. This meant these poor Boston bastards were left with no food, no pot and no booty! Definitely a bad trip for them. Sorry!

We could NOT stop laughing the whole way home. We barreled into our house like a stampede of hyenas. Scott was up watching TV. We were not sure where Greg was. Scott sat at the table with us as we told the whole story. I do not think he could really hear a word we were saying because we were all interrupting each other and talking over each other but he was as quiet as a mouse eating all the snacks we stole.

The next morning, we all woke up in the family room under blankets. It was a bit fuzzy. We must have eaten a ton of food and thought it was a good idea to put in a movie. I was the first to awake to a TV with static fuzz. The five of us were all draped over the furniture or on the floor. I looked around and smiled. I thought it was so cute how close we all were and how well we all got along like brothers and sisters. Scott was the coolest surprise of the house. He is my friend from work. He truly looks out for us, he got along with everyone instantly and ended up being one of the funniest guys I have ever met! He did not say much, but what he did say was dry and full of humor.

He opens his eyes next and mumbles "Hi mamma what's for breakfast?" I said, "Something purchased from the diner, we ate all the food." He giggled and turned to a working channel on the TV. There were food wrappers, empty bags of chips, snacks and trash everywhere. It was really like a cyclone had ripped through our family room.

I stumbled over to the kitchen, started a pot of coffee and sat down at the kitchen table. I cannot believe it was already Sunday and our first weekend was about to come to an end. I did not want to go back to Connecticut. It seems this place is a way to escape from all of my trash back home. I can be a new person, be free from ex-husbands, ex-boyfriends and an ex-life. The life that did not work out for me! When I took out my mental trash last week, after all those years of chasing a life I thought I was supposed to have, I realized I am supposed to make a life of my own. One life that is mine. Not a New Haven life, or a work life or a Killington life. I am going to spend these months creating one life! Filling the pieces of my soul that I threw out with the trash.

Before everyone in the house woke up, I called my roommate, Gwen. She answered the phone "Hey girl, what's up?" I moaned from a very slight hangover. I was more tired than hung over. I told her about my night with the Massachusetts boys and how I stole their food and pot. She was laughing and asking tons of questions. I basically wanted to make sure she was all set moving in and that when I get home tonight from Killington we can start our roommate shenanigans. I smiled when I hung up the phone. I thought, *Wow! Lots of new, cool things happening to me.*

After my five seconds of clearing the day's mental trash it was time to clear the house's weekend garbage. I took out a huge garbage bag and started with the kitchen table. It is like I am possessed by the devil, as soon as I start collecting trash or disposing of it, I get angry and want to kill someone! It STILL reminds me of my ex-husband. The collecting of the trash reminds me of how I would clean the house and overstuff the trash bin underneath our sink. Then I would scream, "Are you gonna WATCH me or actually get the Fuck up off the couch?!" He would start scurrying over to the sink looking at ME like I was a complete bitch wife hag. Ugh! As I am trying to stop thinking about it I look up. Low and behold, there is Scott on the couch staring at me! Looks like some things never change. I mean Scott is not my husband, but he is a man and I grew up with MEN taking out the trash.

Whatever! I proceed to do it myself, walking around him, staring at him as I am cleaning. Then I take my coffee and head on over to my bedroom. Time to pack up and prepare for our trip home tonight. As I am folding and packing my clothes I thought about the snowboarding, the guys, and the fun and just smiled. But I still felt a bit empty. I cannot quite put my finger on it but something is missing. Did I throw too much trash out?

I hear Greg's door open, then a little scuttle up the stairs that was way too delicate to be six-foot four-inch Greg. I peer around the corner and listen up at the direction of the kitchen. I hear a refrigerator, Liza and Robyn talking and Jaime on the phone in the loft. I gaze to my left and see Greg's door open and I can vaguely make out Greg breathing or moving around in his bed. Clearly this person that scurried up the stairs was not Greg and probably not a man. I hear a kitchen chair drag out from under the table and then complete silence. I hear Jaime continue on the phone with her mother and a "Hellooooo" from Robyn. Next a "Good Morning" from Liza. Both in very dramatic sweet yet sarcastic voices. Uh oh, who the hell is in our kitchen?

Robyn and Liza run in my room and are giggling and screeching and cannot catch their breath. I slam the door shut. "What the Fuck is going on right now!?" Liza shrieks, "There is a girl in a black teddy with a coiffed Betty White hairdo. They both start laughing. Robyn squeals, "I can't breathe, who the hell it is?" Suddenly, there is a knock at the door. It is Jaime. I open the door slowly to let her in our secret meeting and she points up to the ceiling and says, "Who the frig is in our kitchen with a nightgown and my grandmother's wig?" I start jumping in place, "Shhhh…oh my God you guys knock it off!"

Very abruptly the door swings open. Greg appears with just his boxers on, sporting terrible blood shot eyes, and hair just sticking out everywhere! "You guys, what the Fuck! I can hear you down the hall, you are such babies, Jesus Christ!" Robyn tried to smooth things over by explaining, "We were just startled by her in our kitchen that's all!" Liza said, "Well I don't frequently run into girls with black negligees on at my kitchen table, sorry to be so immature but she is just sitting at the table making herself comfortable!" Greg barks back, "Her name is Stephanie and she is really nice, do not be a bunch of caddy bitches! Make her comfortable!"

Ok really?? I have to go upstairs and kiss a girl's ass that I never met, who has no problem advertising to a house full of strangers that not only did she come home with our housemate, but she definitely wore and/or PACKED a teddy???? Ridiculous! Then I rationalize, there will be a time when I have someone here and I want my housemates to be friendly, so I will be cool. I give the girls a look that insinuates to knock it off and let's be nice for Greg's sake. We all walk up the stairs and go into the kitchen. "Hellooo, hello again, Good Morning" along with small smiles exchanged by all of us and Stephanie. She immediately became "Stephie" to us. I could not stop whispering under my breath to the girls about Stephie's hair, does she feel a bit drafty in a teddy? Can Stephie at least put on a pair of socks? I was so confused by this girl's behavior my head was about to explode!

While we were all laying around on the couch, "Stephie" finally made her way back downstairs. Scott, who says NOTHING but giggles at us decides to chime in, "It's not like any of us had any game last night." He's right. I certainly thought I had a ton of game but the guys all had girlfriends or were married. I guess the joke was on me. I see what is going on here. Including "Stephie", us girls are always trying to meet guys and want them to stick around. But, guys are just trying to have fun, not marry us! Maybe I am picking the wrong guys? I need to find out with this new pool of available men, what are they looking for? What am *I* looking for? What am I doing wrong? As I am watching this all go down with the "Stephie" hook up in our house, I am thinking, *this girl really thinks we are going to see her again!* The lightbulb just went off! I thought, *what if this is what guys think of me, just a fun night, then I come off all psychotic thinking we are going to see each other again!* I either need to rethink who I am going after or let all that garbage in my head go, and simply have fun like everyone else! But no, that would mean I'm a slut! *Jeeez, this is exhausting*, I thought. I have to just stop thinking and trying so hard! I need to just LIVE!

Anyway, Greg and "Stephie" never returned from the bedroom which was just as well. Scott and Greg were staying an extra night. We just packed everything up and loaded ourselves into the car. All the girls needed to get back by sundown. I will definitely be spending a lot of Mondays off. I was so jealous of Scott and Greg. It would be nice to have an extra night with no rushing and extra time on the mountain. But for the first weekend, I think we did ok.

It was a long ride home. Nothing to look forward to but a long week of work. I actually am thrilled to get home and spend some time with my new roommate. I gaze out the window watching countless trees, hills and mountains and start to think about everything great that will unfold for me over the next few months. It is a beautiful Fall day and the holidays are right around the corner. I think to myself, I will definitely have a boyfriend by the holidays. I mean, now at least I know I do not have to HAVE one, I just WANT one!

Liza rolls on up my long driveway to my beach house. Very small, exhausted good byes are exchanged, and I get my bags out of the car. As I open my screen porch door, I notice Gwen sitting on my couch with a big smile. I welcome her officially and sit down on my comfy chair. Gwen and I immediately start talking about my weekend.

Gwen was very quick to suggest that we can find just as many fun things to do around here and there are a ton of new people in New Haven, we just have to go out, socialize and find them. I agreed. I was up for anything and really feeling good about myself. Gwen and I kept talking about plans for the months ahead, exercising, cooking great food and I was just thrilled that she moved in with me! This was a very intense weekend, full of lots of adjustments as well as adventure! I had just moved into my new ski house and I had a roommate move in with me after being someone's wife! Not to mention countless trash that I threw in the garbage cans every week for the past few years!

Chapter 3

The week was dragging slowly, and it was only Tuesday night. Gwen and I decided to go for a bite to eat at a local restaurant down the street. I was telling her about some guys that I had dated and all the nonsense I had went through in the summer. I also told her about the twin and the Shit he pulled in Killington this past weekend by not showing up. I'm still pissed at him. Gwen said it was my own damn fault. She said I let these things happen to myself. She is right. Maybe it is me? And I am still mad about the toilet paper!

We order our appetizers and sit back and just start talking about nothing. Gwen shares all her secrets with me, as well as funny guy stories. They were all funny encounters at bars and restaurants, but she did not actually do a lot of dating. She is very independent and just does not want to be bothered by all the drama. As she is talking, I notice about an hour has gone by and our table was covered with plates, napkins, bowls, food, bread bowls, etc. It looked like eight people had dined at this table. We start cracking up! Who cares! Well, I did care when I look up at this man coming toward the table, it was this guy I knew from my first job out of college. OH MY GOD! I almost dove on top of the table to hide evidence of all of the food we ate! And where was the Fucking waitress? She has not cleared a crumb since we sat down! I start panicking, he was still as adorable as I remember. He was not from the shoreline, he was from what we call "the other side of the bridge" in New Haven. What the heck was he doing here, on my street? I know it is a free country and people come from all different towns to eat and drink on the shoreline but seriously, not tonight!

"Hey Ella, how are you?" He bends down at booth level and gives me a nice tender kiss on the cheek. "Hi Paul, Paul this is Gwen, Gwen, Paul." Everyone says hello and I ask him how he has been. He explains that he is helping a buddy move down the street and they took a break for dinner. I asked, "um who was that girl you were living with, I cannot remember her name?" Paul explained that they had broken up. I expressed my sincere condolences as I am picturing him in my bed while he is speaking. Gwen is smirking and telling him how we live down the street too. I said, "Where is your friend, if he is moving down the street then we should introduce ourselves, we are neighbors now!" Paul flagged over his friend who was breathtaking, with award winning hair. "Hello ladies, I am Giovanni." He shook our hands very stylishly. Holy Shit! He had a thick Italian accent. Paul explained that Giovanni was at Yale University Medical School this year. He said they had met at a golf tournament this past summer. Well we loved him, and I was still smitten by Paul. It turns out Paul lives close by as well but not on the direct shoreline like Giovanni's house and my house. So, I told them both to stop by anytime they were around. That did not satisfy Gwen, so she started waving her hand back and forth at us and said, "Just exchange numbers this way we can all hang out." Ok, awkward! But it was actually a great idea. So, we did.

The two guys walked away, and I slowly turned to Gwen with this disgusted look and said, "Shit we have at least seventeen plates on this table and I am mortified. We both giggled, and she pointed out that he was Italian. "He's FROM Italy, you people live for food, good God!" She wanted to know all about Paul. There was nothing really to tell. He was my age, apparently single and when I worked way down in Stamford, near New York City, we would all hang out together, go to lunch together etc. Then I had him in a few of my graduate classes at University of New Haven, before I got married. He was a friend and he was living with his fiancé at the time, so I never thought of him in any other way but a friend/coworker. Our conversations were usually about work, school and the occasional advice he needed because he screwed up at home with the girl all the time.

"Did I tell him I was divorced? Gwen, I don't even remember what I said!" She said, "Well obviously you live with me, he knows you are not with anyone serious!" True. Gwen told me to stop overthinking it was a bad habit. Ok well cool, I have his number and I will use it. Maybe he would like to come to Killington sometime. Score!

Gwen and I roll into our beach house, I was stuffed. We both slouched in our regular chair and couch like Edith and Archie Bunker. Our living room is surrounded by gorgeous windows to enjoy the beautiful water views and the gorgeous starry sky over the ocean at night. It is very relaxing. "I'm going to get ready for bed." I got up and went to the back of the house to my bedroom. I put my comfy jailbird pajamas, glasses on and my hair in a bun. The Killington girls always called my pajamas my jailbirds because they were blue and black striped cotton pajamas that looked like a prisoner's outfit.

I come back out and sprawl out in my jailbirds with one leg draped over the chair. The neighbor's house was literally ten feet from ours like every shoreline community. It was so crowded on the water. You can see right in each other's windows! Yep, what was staring at me right in my window was Paul and his friend! "OH MY GOD" I just rolled off the chair and onto the floor screaming, "They are right there, they are right there!" Gwen gasped for air, turned her head but they were already staring at us! She started to wave and said "El, he is coming over here right now!" Noooo, this cannot be, I am in my jailbirds!

There is a scratch and a knock on the screen porch door and I dove on the couch and put a blanket over my body, so you could not really see the whole pajama ensemble. Gwen opened the door and in walks Paul! "That is so crazy, Giovanni lives RIGHT next door to you guys." Gwen and I were smiling and laughing and saying "Wow, how cool!" So, he walks into our family room and sits down at my feet, on the couch. Wow, he is so cute and all I can keep saying to myself is *I have Fucking jailbird matching pajamas on like an asshole right now!*

Gwen wanted to leave us alone, so she went into her room. She did not say goodnight but just excused herself, so it was not obvious. Paul and I had so much to talk about. We naturally had work in common, so we talked about different coworkers we kept in touch with over the years and jobs we have had since we last saw each other. I wanted to know why he was not engaged and living with that girl anymore, but I was not ready to ask just yet.

The small talk was good, and then he pulled my feet up onto his lap. I felt all tingly. He was getting close. We were so comfy. It was nice to be with someone I knew from my past rather than meet brand new people. I hate that awkwardness sometimes. He said, "These are really cute pajamas", as he was rubbing my legs over the blanket. I started giggling and shuttered, "Yea right, stop, they are ridiculous! Hahahaha!" He started laughing and kept trying to lean in and kiss me. He was half laying down next to me on the couch but with one foot still on the floor. He mumbled, "I love your pajamas." My heart was racing a little bit, I was getting excited, but I wanted him to lead. He kept talking. As he was chatting about nothing, I was thinking back to what he was really like back at work all those years ago. Was he cool? Do I care?

As I am trying to think back and remember I am snapped back to life as I hear him say "Yea I am not working right now, speaking of pajamas, I got fired because of pajamas." I replied, "Oh wow really, I'm so sorry! What happened?" He just nonchalantly goes on with "Well I don't have a car, so I was jogging in my pajamas to the train station every day and was using the facilities at the office to shower and change for the day. I figured if I jogged and took the train in my pajamas it would save me from getting two sets of clothes dirty." I could not take my eyes off of him. I was dumbfounded and not talking. All of a sudden, I lost control and let out a laugh and sort of half snort and said "Ok hang on, can you repeat that? You were fired for showering and getting ready at your office because you jogged to the train station and took the train in your pajamas every day?"

Another smirk came across my face, but I was trying not to laugh IN HIS FACE. He said, "Yea we had a gym and locker room in the office building but sometimes if I got to work late and clients were walking in the front door my boss thought it was inappropriate to be walking by them in my pajamas." I could NOT keep a straight face. I wanted to give him the benefit of ANY doubt I had about him being a real weirdo. I mean the reality is, who jogs to the train in pajamas, hops the train IN their pajamas and walks in their office building IN PAJAMAS? But, I was willing to let it slide and not be shallow and picky. I mean he was cute, available and right in front of me.

I just could not put it aside, I needed more information. "Just so I am clear, were they men's pajamas or sweats that you wore to bead? I'm sorry I just need more information." He started sitting up a bit on the couch and got frustrated explaining that he did not really know, basically whatever he wore to bed is what he ran to the train station in. That was not good enough for me, I wanted to know if he wore men's pajama sets or flannels! This was important information that I needed to know, and I knew my girlfriends would ask me.

I just shook my head and said, "Well did you get a verbal and formal warning?" He said, "Well, yea there were a few things." I thought, "Ok, here we go!" I said, "Paul it is none of my business, forget it, so bottom line, you are not working, and you live down the street from me now." He said "Yes, isn't that cool, so I can walk here, walk to Giovanni's and I always eat at the restaurant down the street because I have no car." Oh, that's right! He also has no car. This cannot be good. I got up and kept the blanket wrapped around my jailbirds and walked him to the door. Honestly, I don't even know if he was ready to leave but I had too much for one night. He gave me a big hug and said, "So good to see you and catch up, I will definitely be hanging out here."

Well, I will just keep him on the back burner in case he is fun, and it is something to do. He has no car and no fiancé, so I cannot imagine he is that busy to show me some fun!

***

The week dragged on pretty slowly and I was anxious to pack up and get back to Killington. The girls decided to be on the road by five o'clock pm on this particular Friday. We were in the car talking about work, life, love or lack thereof. I told the girls about Pajama Pants Paul and naturally they were howling in laughter, disgust and disbelief. I kept saying "I have to tell you this Shit, so I remember I'm not in a nightmare!"

Jaime really put a good handle on the conversation. She just put it out there, "Why are we not attracting normal people?" I know the truth is you have to kiss a lot of frogs to find the Prince but honestly, I have kissed every frog, toad, bullfrog, and polliwog on this green Earth. I am "Old Croaker" for Fuck sake! I was trying to explain to the girls that I am fine by myself but always keeping my heart and mind open when I meet new people. I give them a chance and let them in and they have these bizarre issues. I looked out the window and started to wonder if I was putting too much pressure on these frogs and the true Prince I have in my mind is unrealistic. There might just be really nice American Toads out there!

"I just really don't think it is too much to ask." I said to the girls. "I mean I am a normal, pretty girl with a really cool personality. How is everyone else doing it?" I yelled, "Look at Monica Lewinsky, really, she is NOT extremely attractive, and she managed to make her way into the OVAL OFFICE and drop the President's pants! Who does that? I mean how the Fuck did she get in there?" Robyn said, "Girl, I don't know, I wouldn't even be able to get into the janitor's quarters if I had that internship!"

Well, we made it to Killington and decided to stay in for the night. The boys were not coming up this weekend, so we had some extra room, which was nice. When we completely settled in, we all gathered around the fire and started channel surfing for something to watch. I really hope it is not freezing tomorrow. I cannot even admit it right now, but I just do not like snowboarding. If tomorrow does not work out, I am going back to skiing. I look like a flipping idiot out there!

As morning breaks, I am bright-eyed, and bushy tailed from a relaxing night's rest. Everyone is scurrying around making coffee, showering, gathering their stuff for the mountain. We all hop in the car and I immediately suggest we get a half day pass. Everyone jumps down my throat. Sorry, I am not athletic. I am trying sooooooooo hard but let's face it, I am lazy. I would rather a fantastic lunch in a warm bar then freezing my ass off, falling all over the green trails because I suck. It is me and children on the green trails and they blow by me.

Although Robyn and Liza are definitely better than Jaime and I, we all go down the green trail together first. Then I let Robyn and Liza venture off. Jaime and I fend for ourselves and take it a bit slower. I sit on the lift this time. It is not the platter thing, it is an actual lift to the green trails but because you have a snowboard on you have to kind of stand slanted and twisted to keep your board straight yet sit on the lift when it swoops you up. It is the most stressful part of the day, getting on and off these lifts!

I barely make it, but then I have to slide over to the left and just fall so I can secure my other foot in the board. I jump up and do my thing. I am traversing down the first part of the trail. Nice. Nice. Here we go. FALL. Ugh, and this continued ALL DAY LONG. I gracefully fell every three to four feet and my ass was killing me. I lost all my friends, I got so winded, and I could not stand back up. This little Shit who was no more than five years old whizzed by me and said, "ma'am, are you ok?" *Ma'am,* I thought. Yea that is a red flag to get off the Fucking mountain.

I sat up, took my board off and walked down the side of the trail. I was done. The girls would not know if I went all day or down the trail once. I went to sit in the lodge, in the warmth until they were all done. I leaned my board against the building, started tearing my icy gloves and hat off and walked up to the bar.

I ordered a Bloody Mary and just stared up at the television all by myself. Best decision I made all day. I slightly turn to my left and notice a very cute guy sitting next to me. He was also by himself. No ring. Perfect. The next step in trying to pick up a guy is to ease in on the subject of a girlfriend. The girlfriend might have been on the mountain, so you have to tread lightly. I asked him how he made out on the trails today. He was so cute, he talked to me for an hour. He was fairly tall, dark hair and all scruffy in his snowboard gear. Very cute. I told him I was with my girlfriends, we rented a house on the mountain, yada yada. He was from Connecticut, too!

Jaime was heading toward the bar and I flagged her over. She too was exhausted but definitely had more runs than I did. I had a quarter of a run, they went all day. I did not know the guy's name, so I motioned for Jaime to introduce herself. His name was Todd. More small talk was made. We talked about the Connecticut casinos. That seemed to be what we had most in common. He asked me where I was going that night and we both said to meet us at Chatter. He said he was with his friends and they definitely would meet us.

Just as I was watching him walk away, he turned around abruptly and asked for my number. He offered to exchange numbers, so we could find each other this evening. *Oh my God,* I thought. I am so excited. All the girls ended up at the bar by four o'clock. We had a few drinks and headed home to get ready for Chatter.

We had our finest Killington night clothes on and learned from the first weekend when we were dressed like city idiots, that your finest night clothes are jeans, boots and a snowboard shirt. The routine was normal now and we did not feel like we were "new on the mountain" anymore. We walked into Chatter and took our spot in the corner with our Bud Lights. There was a really cool band playing tonight so no matter what happens, the vibe feels like it is going to be a great night.

Liza starts asking me about Todd. I explained he was from Connecticut, liked the casinos, just broke off his engagement, etc. She was excited. She started telling me about some idiot she met on the ski lift that kept screaming "WEINER DOG" at her because she told him she owned a Dachshund. We were cracking up. No sooner do the four of us head to the dance floor and I see Todd and some guys coming in the door. I acted very cool. I wanted him to spot me on the dance floor and not go chase him.

First thing I did was trip down the stairs because I got so nervous that Todd was there. I fell into Liza, and I could not even breathe I was laughing so hard. I said, "Guys he's here! Todd is here!" Everyone just started dancing and acting very casual. Liza kept asking me, "Which one is he?" I was trying not to stare but honestly, I had to think about it. He was all cleaned up in a nice cable knit sweater and hair all styled. He looked like a big pig-pen on the mountain and now I had to make sure I had the right guy.

I found him, and I pointed him out. I put my back to him and continue to dance. Liza shows Robyn and Jaime who he is because everyone is so hard to recognize at night after meeting them on the mountain. The girls are staring, dancing, whispering and laughing. I am not sure what they are talking about, but I just kept dancing and smiling with them. It got a little odd. The girls were crying, laughing and I knew something was off. I said, "Ok what the Fuck is wrong!" Robyn could not speak she was laughing so hard. Liza looked at me and yelled over the music and the crowd, "He has boobs!" I said "What?" She said, "He has a full rack." And cupped her hands in front of her chest to further demonstrate the fact that he had man boobs.

I turned around and got a little upset. In this cable knit sweater he had on, his boobs were sagging. The sweater was clingy, and he had tits. He had a full-on rack! I clearly did not notice it because he was covered with layers of clothing from his snowboard gear. He looked very different this afternoon and much cuter. I yelled at my friends, "OK whatever! Maybe he is really nice! Stop it!" We walked off the dance floor and went up to them. He was really happy to see me. What a great guy! We were laughing and even I was a good sport yelling over to the girls "Boobs McGillicuddy and I are going for a walk." I had to be a good sport, this was supposed to be fun meeting new people, not a job. The girls always set their eyes on prospects too but by the end of the night, they were all taken out with the trash.

At the end of the night, Boobs asked if I was going to be around for lunch tomorrow. I was very excited to say yes I was. We were not leaving until around six o'clock Sunday night. This was perfect. If the girls wanted to go snowboarding again, I would go to lunch with Boobs McGillicuddy. We said good night and planned on talking around eleven o'clock to make our lunch plans.

When we woke up the next morning, the girls were very excited I had a lunch date. When all is said and done, they are always happy for me, we just break each other's balls constantly. That is just the way it is and always will be. If I brought the most perfect man home with the perfect personality, body and job, we would still find something to crack on. You have to be thick skinned and take it.

Everyone left early for the mountain, which left me to get ready all by myself, peacefully. Sure enough, Todd called at eleven and said he would pick me up for lunch. I finished getting ready and waited for his beep.

When he picked me up, he came to the door. It was slightly awkward because he kissed me on the lips. It was very light out and the atmosphere was very different from the lodge and Chatter. So, it was a bit intimidating to be alone with him. He also had a gorgeous jacket on which completely covered any sign of "boobage", so I still had to figure that whole thing out. Maybe the cable knit was just clingy?

We went to this awesome, rustic tavern that was right near the mountain. It was so cozy and pretty. The mountain was very quiet as it was Sunday. We took off our coats and sat in a booth. Yea, no! It was not the cable knit that was clingy, he definitely had a rack. Dammit! I tried to be objective and positive and just continued to be the poised, pleasant little lunch date that Boobs McGillicuddy expected.

The conversation was very pleasant and very mature until after they cleared our plates. As the table was clear, Boobs asked if I wanted coffee or a drink. I said I was good, but we kept talking to try to get to know each other. He said, "Let me ask you this, why are you single?" I told him I had been through a lot and had decided to clear my mind and take some time off from a serious relationship. I explained I had wanted to enjoy my winter and make new friends and be casual. He replied, "Oh, that's great. I am casual too. I am not a love maker or anything. You will never hear me asking you to make love, but you will hear me say I am going to twist your nipples so hard that you squeal like mouse!" And then he started giggling.

I got so completely flustered. I was not talking about nipples I was talking about casual times and new friendships. *What the Fuck is going on right now?* I thought. I wanted to crawl under the table! I half gasped, laughed, clenched my chest and said, "Wow, not what I expected you to say!" He said, "Oh what now you are going to be coy?" I was very confused. I said, "Coy?" He said, "Oh do not be coy when you were the one bringing up being casual." I got a little sarcastic and replied, "I said casual, not one thing about nipple twisting and squealing." I put my hands up, shook my head and could not look him in the face. Ironically, he was the one bringing up nipples with a full rack!

It got very awkward as we got up and left. He gave me a hard time all the way back. I think he felt bad that he said it. And I tried to let it go. I just kept saying "No worries, you said what you said." Meanwhile my nipples actually hurt at the thought of him actually doing that to me. I would be so upset! He walked back inside with me and we sat on the couch. I was trying to finish off the date with dignity. I have made so many stupid mistakes and have said so many stupid things. I wanted to give him the benefit of the doubt. I probably did not want to see him anymore, but I just wanted our goodbye to be peaceful.

Here came the boom. "When do you want to see each other again?" I said, well call me, you have my number. I am usually here on the weekends. He had been on a boy's weekend, so he was not a regular up in Killington. I figured that would get me off the hook from any commitment to make plans. He said, "How about we meet up at the casino sometime?" I said, "Possibly, we will figure it out." He asked, "Do you do rails?" I was sort of confused. I said, "No just craps and slot machines." He looked at me really oddly and said "Ok, I will take that as a no." I really had no idea what he was talking about, I just kept walking him to the door.

I knew the girls would be home any minute and I just wanted him out of there! He leaned in and kissed me. It was a very small kiss. I smiled and said, "Talk to you soon." He then proceeded to grab me, make out with me and he kept trying to bury his knee in my crotch. I think this was supposed to make me feel good but was actually hurting me. He was very intense and breathing as if he NEVER made out with anyone in his life. If I were looking at us from the outside, it would look like he was making out with a tree and wrapping his leg around the trunk. It was gross! The only thing that would have made this more repulsive would have been if I went up his sweater and grabbed his boobs! I was able to pull away and say, "Thank you for lunch, you better go, my roommates will be back soon." He just looked at me with very deep eyes and said, "Ok, talk soon."

I shut the door and leaned against it in complete Fucking amazement. *What the hell was that?* I walked over to the couch and just sat, staring up at the ceiling. I could not help but think that all men are crazy, and it can not only be me meeting these kinds of people. What a roller coaster this is. You get all excited to meet new people, put yourself out there, and then this Shit happens, and you want to hide from the entire world right after the date!

The girls walk in and start with the "How was it how was it!" I told them everything. They kept blurting out gasps or "whaaaaaat" as I was telling the whole story. We were absolutely dying. Liza could not get passed his rack, STILL. And then they said, "Oh and ummm I think rails means cocaine?" Oh my GOD, the guy was asking if I did drugs and I responded, "No just slots and craps!" I buried my head in my hands. I mean I do not do drugs, but that was a really funny response to his question. "Let's get the FUCK out of here", Jaime shouted out. We all thought that was a tremendous idea. I had already been packed so I started to clean as the girls were changing out of there snowboard gear and packing. I was chuckling to myself as I was straightening up, putting dishes away and tying up the trash. I ripped the overstuffed trash bag out of the plastic bin and put it by the door. Boobs McGillicuddy is definitely going out with that bag of garbage tonight!

Chapter 4

I got home pretty late Sunday night and Monday morning was a drag as usual. I am actually excited to stay in with Gwen tonight for cooking and talking. I have not really been relaxing all that much, so I was looking forward to chilling with my roommate. I was dragging myself to the car at five thirty p.m., thinking about how things were going for me. It was cold now and the cold weather reminded me of when Chuck left me a few years ago. I really thought I had taken out my "mental trash" and all the idiots out with the garbage, but I could not understand why I was still dealing with one jerk after the next. Are my expectations too high? Are all single men like this and I am just still being naïve? Did my trash pile up again?

As I am sitting in traffic, my cell phone rang. It was a "number". That means it was not someone programmed in my phone! I would not pick up and I was driving so it would have to wait. As I get closer to my house, the cell phone rang again! It was the same "number". Whatever! I lug my laptop bag, lunch bag, and Kate Spade bag up to the house and pour into the house exhausted! Gwen is sitting at the kitchen table with lemonade and dry corn flakes. I plop myself down at the table and let out a big sigh. Gwen asked, "What do you want to do for dinner? I was thinking of just making a protein shake." I thought that sounded perfect. I replied, "Ya, I actually have protein pouches that I brought home from Killington, they are chocolate flavored, and you just have to put milk or water in them and stir it up!"

I got up and grabbed some cups, ice, water, the pouches, two forks and laid everything out on the kitchen table. The table looked like a lab experiment with two thirty something year old girls too lazy to cook, mixing up our shakes and doing a horrible job. I was sitting at the end of the table with my Solo cup and drink mix rigorously stirring it up with a fork. Gwen is staring at me doing the exact same thing. We are both stirring our shakes with our forks in silence and Gwen says, "How long do you think we have to stir these shakes?" I replied, "I don't know, you are supposed to use a blender, I'm improvising." She said extremely casually, "Oh we have a blender, it's under the sink." What?! My eyes opened really wide and I said, "Gwen if you knew we had a blender why did you just start stirring your shake with a fork, why wouldn't you tell me you bought a blender?" She completely paused, almost put her entire head on the table and cried, "I just followed your lead! I figured if you were doing it, then the recipe must have said stir with fork!" I yelled, "What the FUCK!" I popped up off my seat and retrieved the blender from the cabinet and smoothed out our lumpy shakes with the new blender!

I just could not stop laughing, thinking how dumb we looked stirring our shakes with a fork! We were totally oblivious. Well I never said the kitchen was my strong suit and it is certainly not Gwen's! We calmed down a bit and finished our shakes. The house telephone started ringing, I walked over to the caller id, and it was the "number" again! I turned to Gwen and said "Someone keeps calling me from this number. They called my cell phone too!" Now I am thinking it is a debt collector, maybe? Hmm did I have any outstanding bills? I did not pick up the phone but now I was panicking as to why this "number" was following me around all evening.

After talking at the kitchen table for almost an hour, we cleaned up and went in the family room and sat in our chosen places. Gwen gets the couch, I get the chair. Gwen and I talked so much, sometimes we realize we do not even have the TV on half the time we are together. She was telling me about her Bull Shit weekend, ran into her ex, and how "it sucks being single around here". I was telling her all about

Killington's escapades for the past weekend. Uh oh, it's the phone again. "Son of a bitch!" I yelled. If it is this "number" again I am picking up. Sure, as Shit it was! I answered, "Hello!"

"Heyyyyyyy there, Ella, its Jack from Vermont." I had absolutely no clue who it was. I stuttered, "Hi, what's up?" He proceeded to go on and on about his weekend and the bar was slow Sunday night and I had NO CLUE who the Fuck he was. I was completely embarrassed. He obviously had my cell phone, my home phone and was a slight pain in the ass. Persistent though, I will give him that. He called at least six times on both numbers before I picked up. Huh! Could be my dream man!

He asked me if I was coming up to Killington this weekend and of course I said yes. He said "Cool, stop by the bar." I was giving Gwen a VERY confused scrunchie face and replied, "Yea definitely, see you this weekend." I hung up the phone very perplexed. I turned to Gwen and said, "That was Jack and I have absolutely no idea who he is!" We started trying to piece it together. Ok he said to come to the bar. Was he a bouncer? The bar owner? Bartender? Well I was checking out the bartender at the upstairs bar at Chatter for the past two weekends. But no way, he was HOT! It could not be him. And the name Jack was not ringing a bell. I am such an ASS hole! I gave someone my number, they are calling and seem interested and I have unquestionably no idea who it is.

I called Robyn, no answer. I called Liza, no answer. I called Jaime, "What's up!" she answered. I started the conversation with "Do we know a Jack?" Jaime said, "I'm not recalling a Jack at this moment, but it is possible." I explained what had happened with the phone calls and the chit chat with "Jack". She just could not be bothered. "Nope, sorry can't help you! Hahahaha!" Ok she was of no help to me! Ahh Robyn is calling on the other line. I answered, "Robyn please help me do we know a Jack?" She paused and said, "Yes he is the bartender upstairs at Chatter, you gave him your number Saturday night." I had no recollection. What did I say? Was I acting like a fool? I asked Robyn to please recap. She said, "I don't know what happened, you kept telling me you thought he was HOT and went up to him and was talking to him for a while. He seemed interested. You came back to me and said he just asked for your number." Well apparently, I gave him both numbers! "Ok, thanks I gotta go!" I hung up and recapped all the data we collected on Jack and it vaguely started coming back to me that I was hard core flirting with him and gave him all my phone numbers.

This was actually kind of exciting. I sought this man out at Chatter weeks ago and not only did I have the courage to make conversation with him, but he CALLED ME. He basically hunted me down all day until I picked up. Who does that? He is obviously interested in me! OMG Friday cannot come soon enough!

How cool was this? Maybe things are really looking up for me. I am positive, I am having fun and guys are showing interest in me. I am not acting desperate, I am just being "me" and I am attracting friends, guys and fun times in my life right now. I got up from the chair, continued to talk to Gwen as I was cleaning the kitchen, more so than we had tidied up after the shakes. When I get in these moods, I get a spurt of energy and start cleaning. Let's make room for all the new exciting stuff coming down the trail. It's like I equate it to cleaning up my life, my head and taking out my trash.

***

The car ride back up to Killington the next weekend was a fun one! We all met in the most convenient commuter lot as everyone was working that Friday. Everyone was bitching about work and the trials and tribulations of the week. It was so nice to escape from Connecticut and reality every chance we got. Unfortunately, Scott and George were not going to be coming up again until New Year's Eve due to their work and life schedules. So, it was just us girls.

I had to retell my story about the phone calls and not knowing Jack. The girls were all in agreement that he was hot. And I could not wait to get up to the mountain and go to Chatter. And to think he was calling me! It was a good sign!

This weekend was the weekend before Thanksgiving, so I was very excited to be here. Chuck had left me the weekend before Thanksgiving. Although I took that trash out a long time ago I still cannot help but remember what the weekend felt like. And it is always gloomy outside, cold and I would get a lot of anxiety more so that Christmas was coming, and I was alone. Not this year! No sir! With the way things have been going, I'm sure to be with someone by the Holidays.

We were so tired getting out of the car. This particular drive seemed to be a bit long. We had everything we needed at the house, so it was easy enough to drag in one bag each and sprawl out on the couch to clear our heads and make our plan for the night. Robyn wanted to stay home, and I wanted to go out. Jaime and Liza were indifferent, but I knew I could persuade them my way. I wanted to see Jack! Robyn thought it would be a good idea to wait until tomorrow night to visit Jack at the bar, so I did not look too excited and too available. Umm there are TWO bars on the mountain that everyone goes to and I only have TWO nights here. I had to strike while the iron was hot!

Naturally, I won the battle and we all went out. We freshened up a bit and just headed out, cool and casual with baseball hats on and a laid-back attitude after a long week of work. I walk into Chatter first and there was about twenty people in the whole place. It was after ten o'clock, where was everyone? Well, being that there are only two bars that everyone really goes to on the weekends, The Barn seemed to be the "Friday night bar" and Chatter was labelled the "Saturday night bar." So, this clearly meant I was a loser wanting to run to Chatter. It looked so obvious that I just wanted to see Jack. By the time we could all scramble and figure out that we needed to duck out, I see over Robyn's shoulder, Jack. Jack was waving with both arms, smiling a gorgeous smile and flagging us over to his bar.

"Ladies, how's it going?" Jack said. I was so smitten. I can feel my face getting red and I just all of a sudden got really shy. Liza whispered that we were having one drink with him and then leaving. We got our drinks. Actually, Robyn talked to him more than me because I just for some reason withdrew. I do not know if it was because he was so cute, or I felt awkward that I did not remember giving him my number, but I figured I would let my friends work the magic and break the ice.

I waited by myself as the girls went to the bathroom before we left. I turned to him with a bright smile and started to make small talk. I was leaning over into the bar and he said, "Hey beautiful!" Then he rubbed my arm and I almost lost my balance and slid off the bar onto the floor. I explained to him that we got up here really late. I lied and said we did not feel like hitting the crowded Barn and we just wanted to stop somewhere quiet for a drink. He bought it! Then he said, "Why don't I call you when I get off, around one o'clock, I'm not closing tonight." I said, "Sounds perfect, I'll see you later, definitely."

When the girls got out of the bathroom I was waiting by the door, trying not to look too excited. As we went back out into the cold night I updated them on my progress with Jack. No one wanted to stay out. Now it was still before midnight. I did not care. I figured I would stay up until he called and go back out to meet him. We all went home and put a movie on. The girls got into their sweats and brought blankets into the family room. I sat up straight and tall like a mannequin and waited for Jack to call.

The call came in a bit after one o'clock am. He offered to come over! *How nice is he?* I thought. This is going way to good, I almost had to pinch myself. I gave him our address and waited for him to come over. I woke the girls up and ordered them to their rooms. "Get out of here, grab your items and CLEAR THE ROOM, JACK IS COMING OVER!!!!!" I'm not even sure they woke up, it seemed like, right in their sleep, the girls knew exactly what to do.

I can see the headlights beaming into the kitchen window as he pulled in a parking space. I went to the door and opened it as he was coming down the walkway. He was so freakin cute. He had a completely fit, snowboarder's body, and an adorable little hat that I think is so sexy on guys up here. He had brown eyes, black hair and I had no idea what his last name was.

He walked in and we sat down on the couch. I offered him a drink but he was all set. I left the TV on, so we were completely in the twilight from the TV, with no other lights on in the house. It was perfectly fine. Boy he really brought the cold in. We were trying to get warm. I started to put a blanket over our laps as we were still sitting up, but I was trying to get us cozy. I thought it was pretty forward for a guy to be so open to calling me, seeing me and coming to my house so late at night with not even a first date. He did not really even know me. But, I honestly did not feel awkward because he was so friendly. I just decided to go with it. I figured he lives in Killington, he was a bartender at the most popular bar on the mountain and if he was a real jerk he would have to keep seeing me every weekend. So, I figured, this had to turn out well for me.

I was in the middle of a very dumb story about me and the girls and he just grabbed me in mid-sentence and kissed me. I liked it! It was awesome, and I just went with it. We kissed for what felt like no more than two minutes, then he leaned further into me. He stopped kissing me, moved into a lay down position on my couch, sort of tossing me to the side. I literally almost FELL off the couch! He started reaching for his belt and said very seductively, "How about taking your top off and sucking my dick!" Freeeeeeze Frame! I just completely became paralyzed. My eyes sort of widened, I stuttered, and I said, "Can you just hold on one minute?" I pretended to go to the bathroom. I snuck quietly into Scott's room, because he was not there and had to regroup. I was stunned, pacing the floor and just BURSTED out "What the FUCK!" I was trying to cover my mouth because I didn't want to make noise and then I snorted. I did not know what to do. He does not even know me, he does not know my last name and what gave him the idea that he could say that to me????

I did not know how to handle this because I also did not want this to be completely awkward for everyone for the rest of the season. He was the bartender at Chatter! Just as I regrouped, I went back into the family room. He had one foot off the couch onto the floor and was passed out sound asleep. Ok cool! I figured maybe he was very drunk from bartending all night and he either will not remember or did not really mean what he said. I left him there and went to bed in Scott's room by myself.

The next morning, I heard him leave. I heard steps, the toilet flush and the door slam shut. *Thank God*, I thought. I snuck upstairs without waking the girls. I made coffee and wrapped myself in a blanket on the couch. I was just really shocked. I mean I should not be shocked after all of the dating stories I have, but I thought things would be different now. I took out my mental trash and decided I did not need a man to define me. But I still want a man, I just do not feel like a loser anymore that I went through a divorce and I am single. But I am still willing to have someone in my life.

The girls woke up and all at the same time, they trampled like a herd of elephants into the family room. I was sitting there with a dumb smirk on my face. Robyn tilted her head and looked at me, shaking her head, "What happened?" They all thought because they heard the door shut this morning that something AWESOME happened and wanted to hear all about it. Jaime squawked, "Wait, wait let me get some coffee." Liza just curled up on the couch and under her breath sighed, "This should be good." She knew me and my face all too well. She knew I had a story.

I proceeded to tell them exactly what happened. There were shrieks of laughter, snorting, confusion and yelling all at the same time. I was actually popping out of my seat on the couch with the blanket swaddled around me saying "What the Fuck! I do not understand!" We just could not figure out why someone would have that much gall and ball to come into a strange girl's house and lead with that request!

Robyn tried very hard to reason through this and give him the benefit of the doubt. She kept saying, you know the bartenders, they get hammered behind that bar and he probably did not even know what he was saying. I remembered that I had only left the room for no more than five minutes and when I walked back in to be with him he was passed out. Robyn may have been correct. We decided to obviously not tell anyone. We did not want to embarrass him, and I was going to feel him out later on when we go to Chatter. No one actually felt like snowboarding this time. Which was fine with me! It was so incredibly cold and windy. Sometimes when the wind is really unbearable they close the lifts. We decided to go out and get a really nice hot, delicious lunch and just be cozy for the day.

We texted the usual friends we have accumulated since the beginning of the season, found out who was up for the weekend and told everyone we would meet at Chatter later. We drove up the main access road that leads to the mountain. There are tons of stores and restaurants. We picked a nice, dark, cozy tavern for food and maybe a drink. Everyone got so geared up to RUN out of the car and into the restaurant that we just all flew out of Liza's truck and started running. We walked in huffing and puffing. You could still see our breath inside the lobby! We got a table for four and sat down. As Robyn and I were cackling about onion soup and "Ooooh they have fried mozz sticks", Liza, puzzled, says, "Where's Jaime?" We looked at her empty seat and realized she was not with us. I said, "Oh she probably ran right into the ladies room." Liza's face curled up and she said, "I don't remember seeing her in the lobby." We all sort of looked at each other puzzled. And at the same time, we ALL got up out of our seats, dragged our big wooden chairs out from under us, making the usual spectacle of ourselves. We ran outside and saw Jaime, with both palms pressed up against the backseat window scathing pissed. We got out of the car so fast, Liza locked her in before she could open her side!

I do not think I ever laughed so hard in my life. She was not happy with us. But it was an honest mistake. She was yelling at us, "How could you get ALL the way into the restaurant, SIT DOWN and realize I was not there! My whole life flashed before my eyes, I thought I was going to freeze and DIE!" Naturally everyone was staring at us as we made our way back to the table. It was one of those moments where everyone was wiping their eyes from tears of laughter, sighing and breathing hard. Only us! So, there we were, finally, settled in ready to order lunch. And the lunch talk begins, naturally with the topic of Jack.

As I am feeling sorry for myself, Liza said something pretty profound. She said, "Do you think it is the guys you are picking? Or you might be assuming any guy who pays attention to you is the guy for you. Some guys are going to be great and the other eighty nine percent will definitely be assholes." She was on to something. Maybe I was not being very selective. I mean I literally see a guy and if they pay attention to me I am in and if they do not, I obviously move on to the next one. But maybe I should be the one doing the picking. I should be the one doing the screening. How could I be so shocked at Jack when I literally do NOT know him? I think it might be time to start doing the choosing or at least not be so shocked at guys' behavior. My expectations of men being gentlemen must still be too high.

Our soups were served, and Robyn was trying to explain the difference in the types of guys out there. "You are going to get what you pick!" It's like knowing the quality you are going to get if you shop at Walmart and not Nordstrom. If you continue to shop at Walmart and be surprised that your clothes are not made as well as your Nordstrom outfits, Walmart is not on the same level as Nordstrom. Ella, ya need to start shopping at Nordstrom's." I gave her such a harried look and said, "Robyn, I'm not even in a store! I am at a flea market on the side of the road or a tag sale!" Ugh! It's just so Fucking frustrating.

I really stopped and got really quiet through lunch. I am listening to these three girls who are just as smart, successful and single as I am. They each have their own stories and have been meeting guys. They just do not talk about it and do not really have things happen to them like I do. Am I still picking the wrong types of guys? Did I think one trip to the curb was going to clear my mental trash out for good? Maybe I am not as "cured" as I thought I was with this whole wanting a man thing. We can make tons and tons of trips to the curb with our trash. The more trash we accumulate the more needs to be taken out. Maybe I am still bringing the wrong kinds of men into my life. I do not need a man, but I want a man. It should not mean ANY man. *Honestly, garbage in IS garbage out,* I thought.

***

I thought a lot about my new revelation all day this particular Saturday. I am glad we had a peaceful day off from the mountain. Everyone was quiet either reading or watching a movie. I was in the family room watching a movie with Robyn and Jaime but not really watching. My mind was wandering. I was excited. At least now I recognize issues I am having, and I want to do something about them. I do not just blame everyone else for my issues or think they will magically disappear as they did when I was a child.

This was a great thing! I think I took my own trash out in my head just now which is clearly more valuable then tossing all the guys out with the garbage! My clear head got me grounded and excited. I am still wanting to be with a man, which is different from needing a man. Now, I am conscious of at least getting to know if they are right for me, instead of assuming they are right for me. I realized I do not have to act on every man I see!

After two movies, drifting in and out of a nap and catching up on some texts, we started to rally for sushi and Chatter. Tonight was going to be fun and I told the girls that I was willing to give Jack the benefit of the doubt. And if I want to have fun with a guy, knowing he is an idiot, it is my prerogative. After all, while I am looking for Mr. Right, what is wrong with having a Mr. Right Now? Or how about NO man at all!!

Off we went into the icy Saturday night. Sushi was great. More laughing about nothing, bantering and blubbering girl talk. Thank God Robyn was talking about the guy SHE met last night from Chicago. He and his friends were here for a ski trip and she said she would meet him for some drinks. We all focused on that for a change. Liza and Jaime really could have cared less if they met a guy or not. That was not why they joined in on the ski house. They were always indifferent and off causing some kind of trouble at the bars like finagling free shots or stealing something from the band.

Chatter had a line out the door and it was the coldest night of the season so far! Once we hit the cover charge and coat room I was more than ready for a Jägermeister to warm my blood! I was not ready to go upstairs to look for Jack. I needed to have a few drinks in me first to face him and his dick sucking comment. It was really a great night at this bar as everyone was really not returning back until after Christmas. There were tons of people and two really great bands.

We made friends with one of the girl bartenders on the first floor as we were sucking drinks down to warm up. She made a comment about how "her and Jack are switching bars in an hour because he didn't think it was fair that he was always upstairs." I said, "Oh you know Jack?" She said "Yea great guy, really messed up but great guy. He's gotta stop doing pills man." Oh jeeeeeez. I almost died. Ok, well that is good to know. And considering I did not know him at all and still do not know his last name, I might have been a little more careful inviting him into my home last night. Liza and I were screaming over each other as the music was so loud. I was trying to figure out why he was calling me all week? Liza said, "He liked you, nothing wrong with that, just do not keep your wallet or prescriptions around him and you will be all set." NOT FUNNY!

Finally, I gathered up the nerve to go upstairs to see Jack. And I did not even care anymore because now that I knew what the girl said about him, he seemed vulnerable to me, almost pathetic. Wait nope, when I got to the top step and glanced over at him he looked completely Fucking hot! I did say there was nothing wrong with a Mr. Right Now! I went over to him and he acted like nothing was wrong. He looked a little messed up. He said, "Hey girl, sorry I bailed this morning, I don't even remember falling asleep." I said, "Did you know where you were when you woke up?" He threw his head back, "Of course I did!" I smiled and just walked away. This guy is harmless. And if he wants to hang out and I have nothing to do, I will hang out with him.

The night was pretty uneventful, and I wanted a large pizza and my couch by one o'clock in the morning. This was a great scene and I would not regret being here for anything. I am just kind of glad we are not coming back until New Year's Eve because it gets monotonous every weekend. It will be a nice break and I will have something to look forward to in a month.

I went upstairs and said good bye to Jack. He said, "I'll keep in touch beautiful, have a safe trip back tomorrow." OMG, I love him! We went home with two pizzas and brownies. We recapped the uneventful night. Robyn was talking to the guy from Chicago and it was basically a bust. He told her he would love to take her out sometime. Then he walked away from her and she saw him leave. He never asked for her number, so she will never ever see him again. He probably was married for all we knew. He was probably on a guy's weekend and wanted to see if he had any game. Then he probably chickened out when he realized, "*Duh I'm married, and my wife will remove my balls and stuff them in her purse if she ever finds out I'm talking to a girl!*"

On Sunday we woke up and cleaned the entire house because we were locking it up for a few weeks. I brought a lot of stuff home to wash and we made sure all of the groceries were not left with expiration dates. We hopped in Liza's truck and left. We were all in good spirits as we had another great weekend together in breathtaking Killington. There was never a reason to complain. We laughed a lot on the way home. The conversation for the last hour was a full analysis of how we could have possibly left Jaime locked in the truck and how Jaime could not find a way to unlock it from the inside.

I got home at a decent hour, which was nice. Gwen was doing laundry. She was dying to tell me about a guy she met that owns a restaurant and she had a great time all weekend with him. Nice! I pay one thousand dollars and travel six hours, roundtrip, every weekend and I only had a story about some guy saying, "Take your top off and suck my dick."

After I told her the "Jack" story and the "Jaime getting locked in the truck" story, I started to tell her about my reflection and how I am aware now of assessing whether or not someone is right for me, instead of assuming I will mold everyone into being the right one for me. I also told her that now I am aware of this and it doesn't mean I can't have a Mr. Right Now to amuse me while I am searching for Mr. Right. She agreed and might want the same thing. So, we started a list of everything we want Mr. Right Now to be. The list was compiled, and we went over it one more time.

> *He doesn't have to call.*
> *He doesn't have to take us out on dates.*
> *He is a secret, a dirty little secret.*
> *He is STRICTLY an affair, no feelings.*
> *He can only come over once maybe twice a week.*

If it becomes drama or we start to have feelings for him, we get rid of him.

This was starting to really seem like a good idea. Gwen said, "Mr. Right Now will just amuse us and buy us time until the right one comes along." I said, "Excellent, and we will call him *Phil*, for *filling* up our time!"

Chapter 5

As the thought of "Phil" set in, Gwen and I prepared for a long holiday season. One day flowed into the next with work, temperatures getting colder and calendars filling up with holiday parties. It seemed my calendar was filling up but not "Philling" up! I wanted this holiday to be free from sadness, mourning lost loves and pining over what I had and be a big celebration of what I have coming to me. I tried really hard not to think about it and I NEVER practice what I preach or think.

Gwen and I planned a night in to decorate our Christmas tree and have some dinner. I walked into the house after another mundane Thursday of work. There were four or five cans on the kitchen counter, which struck me as odd, but I just do not ask anymore. Gwen was already lugging boxes from outside storage into the house. The tree, the ornaments and all the other random decorations were starting to come to life around our little beach house.

As the tree was going up, I got a little anxiety. I kept thinking about decorating my tree when I was married and now I am decorating a tree with a roommate. It is like I am going backwards. Then I threw that thought away in my mental trash can and came back to reality recognizing the fact that my husband chose to go out with his friends at the exact time we started to decorate our tree and would leave me alone. I guess what is happening now is actually taking a step forward.

I was getting really hungry and asked Gwen what her thoughts were for dinner. She said she was trying to do pasta fagioli (*fazoooool*), but the can opener was not working. I asked her if that was the reason for the five cans of cannellini beans laying on our kitchen counter. She was really annoyed, "El, I bought this new can opener and it just does not work. I kept trying to open cans like the lady said at the dem I bought it from and it is like it has no blade. It WON'T open any of the cans." I walked over to the cans and tried it myself. I sat the can opener blade atop the can. I started grinding, winding and grunting as the can seemed to be spinning clockwise. Still, the opener was not cutting the tin, and nothing was happening. *What the Fuck is going on?* I thought. Gwen and I stood at the can opener and can of beans completely confused as to why this thing would not cut the tin can at the top. I grabbed the beans and can opener and said, "We need some help!"

On this particularly windy night on the beach, Gwen and I walked over to our neighbor, Giovanni's house. Giovanni is our neighbor that we met at the neighborhood restaurant with Pajama Pants Paul. We knocked on the door and over walks the dreamy Italian with a t-shirt and flannel pants on. He looked so cozy and sexy at the same time, I just wanted to curl up next to him on the couch in a pretzel formation!

"Hello ladies, what's up?" As Giovanni opened his screen door slowly, we wiggled inside because it was absolutely freezing. We asked him if he could help us open our can of beans. I started getting ethnic on him. "Giovanni we are making the pasta fazooool." He looked up and sort of smirked but looked very confused. He put the can opener under his arm, put his hand on the top of the can, looked up at us in a bit of a disgust and lifted the lid. We were SILENT! I said, "Oh my God, I don't understand?" Gwen was just giggling and nervous and confused. Giovanni informed us it was a side cutter.

So, this Yale Medical student thought we were complete idiots and certainly could not make our way around a kitchen. We made a huge joke out of it and thanked him, and he was a very good sport. "Sorry to bother you!" we yelled as we waved good bye and escaped off the porch. We were running back to our house and I said under my breath with clenched teeth, "Do not say a word until we get in the house I am Fucking dying right now!" We were embarrassed as we poured ourselves back into the house. I could not stop laughing, Gwen was ornery because it was her mistake. She started picking up all the cans, they were ALL opened. They were ALL opened because she kept trying and trying on all of our cans thinking we had a busted up can opener.

We managed to march on, finish the tree and cooked dinner. We were both sort of eating and talking and looked as if we just ran a marathon over the exhaustion of the tree and the can opener saga. As I was taking my last few bites of the fazool my phone beeped. It was a text. "Hey m'lady." I was confused. I picked up the phone, opened up the entire text and it was from Don. Don was the guy I dated from Atlanta last year who took me to an arcade and spoke in the third person. I looked up at Gwen with disgust. "It's Don from Atlanta, what the hell does he want." Gwen immediately perked up, "Stop thinking everyone is your next serious relationship. He could be a Phil, you are supposed to be thinking casually, write back, and see what he wants…" OK!!!

I replied to his text. We bantered back and forth, and he basically told me he was coming home in a few days for the holiday season and wanted to get together. I supposed it could not hurt. It was something to do right? I told him to definitely contact me when he was in town and we would get together. I looked up at Gwen after the texting stopped and she was very proud of me. I guess I always immediately think of a guy as the "one" and this new *Phil* situation will keep me aloof and not worrying about so serious all the time.

Our house looked so cute with all the Christmas decorations and I was feeling very festive! The holidays were hard last year, and I am really looking forward to a nice season, as Christmas is my favorite time of the year. I went into the living room which was lit up only with Christmas lights. It was so peaceful. Gwen insisted on washing dishes, so I just lumped myself over my Archie Bunker chair and started texting again. My fingers navigated over to Don and I continued to text with him.

ME: "So is it warm down there?"
DON: "Don is warm, yes?"

Oh no here we go, he even texts in third person. I remember at the adult arcade last year he kept talking in the third person and very robotic. Like syllable by syllable. WHY am I texting this kid right now? What is wrong with me?

No sooner do the texts start flowing in all night from Pajama Pants Paul who found out from Giovanni that we were incapable of operating a side cutter can opener. Pajama Pants Paul and I were going back and forth, and he was starting to grow on me. *Another Phil*, I thought. My only concern is going backwards but I promised myself I would have a light, drama free holiday season. But the worrying is NOT stopping. It has to stop. I cannot worry about going back to the past and just enjoy each day in the now.

The rest of the week went by and the craziest ghost from my past was texting like a fiend. It was the Twin! I have not spoken to the Twin since he was on his way up to Killington with toilet paper. I am hoping he was trying to make amends for what he did to us. It was rude. He is so cute though, I feel like I need to see him. I need to understand what is going on with this one. As the texting went on about nothing, I realized it was time to wrap up and enjoy the weekend, as I was at work. I got up the courage to ask him what he was doing this weekend. He said he was working all night. He wanted me to contact him after eleven o'clock, when he would be done. Oh boy! I ended up going home after work and figuring out what I wanted to do to amuse myself until eleven o'clock. Gwen was out with coworkers. Later on, I knew I would have to pretend I was out at eleven o'clock, even if I was sitting home. I was afraid if the Twin knew I was home he would say "Stay in, I'll talk to you soon." So, I just stayed in, watched TV and texted with Don until the clock struck eleven.

I wanted to be cool, so I waited until twelve after eleven. I figured I would be aloof in the time and just make it random to show I was not waiting. I shot a text *Hey are you out.* I jumped up and ran down the hallway to my room, so I can get ready and fix my make-up. Sure enough, DING, he replied! *Hey yea heading to Bottega Bar, swing by.* My heart sunk. YES! I wrote back that I was finishing up with some friends and I would be by "in a few".

If he ever knew I got my ass out of a comfortable chair on a freezing Friday night at eleven o'clock just to see him I would absolutely die. I fixed myself, I looked gooooood. And off I went to meet him. It was so cold, I was shivering in the car. I was also kind of tired. But the adrenalin of meeting the Twin kept me pumped up and I headed into the city to find a parking spot.

I was okay with walking in alone because he thought I was out with friends and split up from them. So, I proudly pranced over to the entrance and handed the bouncer my I.D. I paid a ten dollar cover and stepped into the dark, steamy club. It felt really good to be warm and cozy. I looked around a bit and did not see him. I walked over to the bar and waited for a drink as to not look like I was searching for him. In the corner, I see a crowd of people, some of which I recognized as his friends. I carefully continued to glance over and caught a glimpse of him. And yes, it was really him, not his twin.

I walked over with my drink and sort of stood to the side until he saw me. When he finally saw me, his face lit up and he broke through his circle to come over to me. He gave me a kiss on the cheek. We had idle chit chat for a bit. The music was loud, so it was not really easy to have a conversation. Then finally he said, "I'm really sorry about what happened a few weeks ago with Vermont." He didn't really explain anything. Just that he was sorry. I was wondering if he turned around on the way up or was he lying the whole time and never left to drive up. I instantly stopped the wondering, smiled and said, "Oh it's completely fine, you know me I could care less." I always try to paint myself as "chill". He kissed me on the cheek again. It was a slow kiss on the cheek then he dragged his lips to my neck and out came the mmmmmmmmmmmmmm".

We had a great time at the club as if nothing had ever happened. It did cross my mind that Liza and the girls were going to KILL me, but this is what girls do. We state our opinion, know our girlfriends will not listen and then are right there to pick up the pieces that we know eventually will fall. I went to the bathroom. When I got back I saw him talking in a crowd. There were a few new people that had not been there all night. I did not know anyone else there but him, and I did not want to be needy. I started talking to this girl in the crowd and kept one eye on the Twin the whole time.

It was getting late. Very close to last call. He was talking to this little bitty of a thing with gorgeous long hair. The girl looked prepubescent! I was getting really annoyed. Now, I decided to prey like a red-tailed hawk around this situation. He was just ignoring me. There were people around us who had been making small talk with me. The girl I was talking to asked, "Are you coming to after hours?" I asked where and she told me it was at the Twin's house. Interesting that he is having an after-hours party and did not invite me yet. I am sure I am being paranoid. He would not have asked me to come down to this bar if he was going to ignore me. So, I snuck up behind him as he was talking to baby-alive and I tapped him. He turned quickly, put his finger up and said, "Hang on a minute." He looked completely annoyed at the interruption.

I shouted over his shoulder, "What's going on after this?" He turned around and said quickly, "Everyone's coming back to my place, you are welcomed to come." Ok, so I think I am just being paranoid and I do not want to look like a nut. So, I graze out with the rest of the late-night cattle when the last call lights turned on. I buddied up to the girl that I had been talking to and sort of followed her there. She was in the garage across the street from my car. We were comfortable in knowing that we were leaving at the same time. Girls do that!

It was a very short ride to the Twin's house, thankfully. I pulled up to his house at the same time most people were pulling up. I could not believe how forward I was going to the bar by myself and now his house by myself not knowing any of these people. I was glad I had expanded my confidence and ability to go out and get what I wanted. As I was lifting my head back up from the cold chilling walk up the path, I landed at the front door only to find the Twin in the hallway with the little pre-pube! What the Fuck!!!!!!

I walked in fat, dumb and happy. I did not want the Twin to see me sweat. I walked right up to him. He said "Heyyyyyyyy, there she is. Go in and get a beer, chill out. My work friends are really cool." I did just what he told me to do. I sat on the couch and laughed and socialized and talked. He was with the youngster and I saw them disappear. I could not take it anymore. I was really starting to get upset. I wanted to go home, I wanted to talk to him, and I wanted to understand why he invited me out in the first place.

I got up to get a beer or so the party goers thought. But I was slick. I walked out of the kitchen and down the hallway. I had obviously been to his house before, so I knew which bedroom door was his. It was shut. They were all shut. I did not want to be caught in the hall, so I scurried into the bathroom. I pulled myself together as I was shaking a bit. I refused to leave that party until I saw him come out of the bedroom! I went back into the main room and acted like nothing was wrong. I was talking, laughing, and watching some drinking games. No one seemed to care who I was. Everyone assumed I was with someone else.

Sure, as Shit, the Twin appeared in the kitchen with sweats on and slightly disheveled hair. The little girl was nowhere to be found. Still in his bed, perhaps? Who knows? I sprung off the couch, into the kitchen. He looked over at me approaching as I approached him. He tilted his head to the side and said, "Hey so glad you came, are you having a good time." I said, "Yea I'm having fun, where did you disappear to?" He said, "Well my friend was not feeling well so I was in the other room, listen I'm sort of seeing someone, I hope we can be friends and there are plenty of guys here that are really cool, I want us to be friends. That's why I invited you out tonight."

My heart beat directly out of my chest and up my throat. I felt my face getting hot and I really could not even see him all that well through the nausea. I said, "Oh I had no idea, oh ok, no that is fine." He said, "Well I wanted to break the ice after the Killington thing. I figured you were out, so it would be good to stop by and have a drink together." I was nodding, "Yea, no of course, totally fine!" I said and put my head down. I was trying to act so cool. I looked up at him and said, "Well you don't have to worry about getting your girl pregnant since she probably hasn't gotten her period yet, good luck!"

I smiled a crazy smile and walked out. It was so cold, I trotted to my car, got in, and just started sighing and shaking my head. I was actually talking to myself mumbling, "You gotta be kidding me!" As the car warmed up I just drove away.

It was three o'clock in the morning! I was so tired, I was nice and cozy in my chair earlier at eleven o'clock that night. Why did I go back? Why did I fall for that? I felt like SUCH a loser. He was not even a contender to be a *Phil.* I totally called that wrong because I am STILL being an idiot!! Now I'm recycling OLD trash!!

I get home, get in bed, very quietly. I was trying to fall asleep and I just envisioned myself as a homeless bag lady sifting through the dumpster pulling out Pajama Pants Paul, Don from Atlanta and the Twin. I had it all wrong. Keeping it casual through Christmas digging up ghosts from my past, having a "Phil". WRONG! If they sucked the first time, what would make them be good guys the second time around. I do NOT want to keep going backwards. Why was I recycling trash just because of the holidays? I closed my eyes, and thought to myself, *remember please, never get burned by the same yule log twice!*

Chapter 6

Christmas came and went. My family had an absolute ball together. A simple Christmas Eve meal for twenty-seven and a Christmas Day feast for thirty was enjoyed, along with a lot of homemade red wine! Liza and Jaime spent the holidays with me as they are family. We were just in the corner for two days drinking and laughing. Made it through, merrily! We left for Killington on Christmas night with Robyn in tow. Our holiday break in Killington was planned for ten days. This was supposedly the best time in Killington according to the locals and renters. We had New Year's Eve planned for Chatter and took the rest of the agenda day by day.

The first day was kind of cool. We got up early and went to the mountain. It was nice to see everyone from the ski houses, as it had been a long holiday season without being up there. I know I took an oath about recycling men, bringing in the wrong garbage, but damn, Jack, the bartender, looked HOT in his snowboard gear. He looked all shabby snowboard chic, with is dark brown, unkempt hair and delicious unshaven face! He came right up to me when we were getting ready to hit the lifts. He asked me what I was doing all week. I said for him to call me and we would hang out. I think he was drunk or definitely on something. As soon as he slurred, "Why don't you head over to the bar tonight", he tripped over his foot with one foot fastened to his snowboard and fell toward me. I went to catch him, and his helmet hit my cheek! OUCH! What the Fuck, you pill popping klutz!

Liza turned around, completely disgusted and said, "Did he ask you to take your Under Armour off and suck his penis?" I said, "No, and stop it, he was really out of it that night and might have regretted saying that, I need to give him the benefit of the doubt!" Jaime just shrugged her shoulders and said, "You're an idiot but okay, HA!" And away we went into the clouds for another debacle of a day on the trails!

Let's see, I did about three runs to everyone else's seven because I SUCK! I pulled my gear off and went into the lodge, early, like I do every time I am snowboarding. I went to the bar in the Killington Base Lodge to get a signature Bloody Mary and to my right was this really cute, very Italian looking guy. He was not terribly tall, had dark olive skin and your typical over thirty, hot boy, brown hair. He was wearing black ski pants, a red, Under Armour turtleneck and I could see his cut body underneath the shiny layers. Holy Shit!

We were both staring up at the television above the bar and he leaned over and said, "This is much better in here then out in that cold." I looked at him and smiled. I was trying to play it cool, he was not going anywhere. He had a brand-new drink in his hand, so I was trying not to be annoying talking to him every five seconds. I was making buttons though! I wanted to talk to keep the conversation going soooo badly! I looked over the bar, out the glass walls to see Robyn and Liza dragging ass into the lodge. They were chit chatting about certain runs, the yard sales they had, laughing, etc. I put my hand up and widened my eyes, demanding silence. I slowly tilted my head to the right where the Italian snow dream was standing with his drink. They immediately took on their roles as wing girls and started circling near him, ready to help me go in for the kill.

They were talking to him for a while, I was standing a little over to the side. I did not want to be aggressive. Robyn turned my way and said, "Ella he is really nice! He's getting divorced, he is actually from Connecticut, not far from us, and you need to talk to him." I slithered into the circle and started picking up the conversation they were having about "what mountain they like better". I have no idea, I just start making up Shit. *Oh yea, I love Mad River Glen! Stratton is my favorite!* Bull Shit, I have only been to Killington. Whatever! So, Robyn and Liza, nonchalantly, turn to the bar and stood side by side away from our conversation. I asked him what his name was, it was Dennis. Okay that is not very Italian, but he obviously was partially Italian. After mindless banter about snowboarding, and Connecticut restaurants we have been too, I got out of him that his mom was 100% Italian. There ya go!

So, I rustled up enough nerve to ask him what he was doing up in Killington over the Holiday. He said he and two buddies decided to come up to the mountain for New Year's Eve. Bamm! He was going to be here for the next four days. I said, "Well my name is Ella, we have a rental up here so if you want to meet us, or need to know where to go, just find us." He smirked and said, "Well how about I take your number." I pulled the old *call me, so it comes up on my phone.* Bad move, now I have his number and I better not submit to the drunk dial tonight!

Jaime finished up with her run and wanted to leave when she got to the base lodge, so we got out of there late afternoon. When we got back, we all got warm, made tea and regrouped on the couches. It was nice to have the house all to ourselves with no guys. Scott was coming up for New Year's Eve but could not make it the entire week. We never know where George is and quite frankly do not really care. So, we all sprawled out on the couches and started dishing about Dennis. Liza told me she thought she heard him say he had kids. Robyn recapped that he was going through a nasty divorce and I did not care because I had his number and knew he would definitely call me over the next few days.

The next few days actually proved to be pretty routine and drama free! Get up, watch movies, maybe or maybe not go to the mountain, eat dinner, shower and go to The Barn or Chatter. We definitely had fun and got drunk every night, but it was very uneventful. I never heard from Dennis and I also never ran into Jack. New Year's Eve morning was upon us and I knew it was going to be the night of all nights. I was excited to take my years' worth of garbage out and made a promise to take no more garbage in!

We were relaxing that morning and heard Scott come through the door. We all jumped up and ran screaming "Scotty Too Hottie!" It was so great to see him. He brought his stuff in, came into the room and we caught him up on all of our shenanigans of the week. He had a tremendous idea! "It's New Year's Eve, it's foggy, the lifts will probably close, let's bar hop all day and end up at the party at Chatter." Excellent idea! We all popped up and got ready for the day. I made everyone promise not to get too banged up because I wanted to come home before Chatter, shower, get pretty and call a cab.

It was eleven forty-five a.m., and our first stop was the Killington Base Lodge. Even though we did not snowboard it was still cool to go to the lodge in regular clothes and hang out. A lot of people we knew were there. We had our typical Bloody Mary good time. Jaime and I were starving so we talked the group into going to the nice cozy tavern where we love the onion soup and had locked Jaime in the car by accident.

We piled in Liza's truck and headed over to the tavern. It was kind of balmy and foggy for a New Year's Eve day. Very odd for Killington, but unseasonably nice for a change. We got our table for five and settled in. I switched to beer at this point and the girls started drinking vodka. Uh Oh! Not sure what Scott was drinking but we camped out for a while. We were talking about how Shitty the year was. If I recall, every New Year's Eve I talk about how Shitty the year was and how I am cured. I talked about my revelation of wanting a Mr. Right Now or a *Phil,* as Gwen and I called it. But the reality of it was, nothing changed, I am still taking in the garbage as much as I hate taking it out!

Naturally, my ex-husband came up. The girls started reminiscing about how funny he was and telling random stories. I was giving them such a cross, confused look that read *Shut up!*

I yelped, "Excuse me, I'm still in the room and don't feel like talking about him!" Robyn said, "He was just so nice and so funny." I said, "I'm sure Charles Manson had a good side to him too. I bet he was a real hoot and made everyone laugh in the prison! I don't want to Fucking hear it anymore!" Heads nodded, point taken!

Now, the stroke of four o'clock p.m. came upon us and I was itching to go home, rest, make sure I ate dinner and got all spruced up for Chatter. In my head I knew I would see Jack, maybe Dennis and a whole new crew of people who just got in for the New Year's celebration. We rallied and paid the tab. No one was really drunk but we were very silly! The conversation ended up all about Scott. We grilled him about girls, about what guys think and how we should react to certain things. Scott basically said that most woman are crazy. He also said that women are stalkers because they call and text. So basically, I gathered that no matter how much social media we have now, and it is very easy to communicate freely, men are still the hunters and they still like to chase. As soon as the words were running through my mind like a stock ticker, I had my phone in my hand texting Dennis. So much for the chase!

ME: *Hey it's Ella from CT, you having fun this week?*

Let's see what he says. I want to see if he is coming to Chatter, is that soooo psycho! He asked me for MY number, so he was interested.

We all get back to the house and I ran right into my room and started getting ready. *DING*

DENNIS: *Hey! Yea, going.*
ME: *Cool let's meet up for a drink.*
DENNIS: *K*

Wow, Dennis is not so talkative. Anyway, I was psyched. I just met him this week. Not sure if I'm taking in garbage but sure as hell am not recycling it and that is a good thing.

Everyone kept their buzz on in the house with a beer and rallied back into the living room to wait for a cab. The cab shows up, headlights gleaming through the window and off we went. When we got to Chatter there was a line around the parking lot like I had never seen before. This long line equaled a long night of fun! We got in line and luckily it was not that freezing. We got in and out of line talking to friends we had seen that afternoon. I was trying to finagle us a better spot in line, but no one was falling prey to my charm. By eight thirty p.m. we were in. The cover charge is sixty dollars! I am getting every penny worth of fun out of this night.

Chatter was covered in festive decorations and the bars were draped with New Year's hats, crowns, boas, rings and noisemakers. Liza and I ran to the bar and just started dressing ourselves, dressing Robyn, Jaime and Scott and we were just submerged in New Year's Eve fun. There were bands upstairs, downstairs and additional makeshift bars to keep up with the crowd. Scott went completely missing. I feasted my eyes on a Jägermeister station in the far corner and dragged the girls over to it. We did our first shot of the night, each chased by a Bud Light.

Next stop was the dance floor. The main headliner band was so incredible, we could NOT stop dancing. Every time we tried to get off the dance floor was another "Oh my God this is my FAVORITE." As we danced, we each took turns running to the bar to get rounds of shots and beers. I would say at this point I was five shots in, five beers in and that did not count the alcohol I had during the day. I was getting fuzzy and feisty. We decided to take a break to go upstairs. Low and behold, Jack was behind the bar upstairs. He is so damn cute, I smile every time I see him, even though he is a pill popping klutz who bruised my cheek and asked me to take my top off to blow him.

We went over to Jack's bar and got four more beers. There was a really cool band playing and the atmosphere was slightly more subdued. We walked over to the balcony to look over at the main dancefloor. There was Scotty Too Hottie dancing with two busted girls. We were screaming from the top floor and cutting our throats with our hands yelling "NO! Too Hottie! NO! Run away!" He saw us, looked at the girls and just walked away right in the middle of the dancefloor. Sorry girls!

It was getting late enough that we had to watch the time but it was not so close to midnight yet. I wondered where Dennis was.

> ME: *You here*
> DENNIS*: Decided to drink in…long day*
> ME: *booooooo*
> DENNIS*: lol, we will catch up soon*
> ME: *text later if you feel like leaving you house bored*

I clearly cannot text when I'm drunk because that made no sense. I had hit send and was having so much fun I could care less! I did feel a bit of disappointment that Dennis was not coming to Chatter. To numb the pain, I went over to Jack's bar. I ordered a beer and a shot all by myself. He was hammered too! It was just ugly at this point. Everyone was out of their mind and midnight was approaching. I had no idea where to find my friends and wanted to kiss someone at midnight.

I was three feet away from all of my friends on the upstairs dancefloor but did not realize it because I was out of my mind. When I realized they were right in front of me, I raised both my arms to get their attention and waved them over. They bounced over and I was screaming, "It's almost midnight. Everyone stay CLOSE TOGETHER!" They grabbed three more beers. Liza went over to the balcony and spotted Scott. She got his attention too and thank goodness by midnight, we were all together, upstairs at Jack's bar. At about three of midnight, we lined up new beers and one shot each. When it got to be two minutes until midnight, the place was roaring with horns blowing and screaming.

Finally, at midnight, we screamed, hugged, kissed, did our shots and started jumping around. As I turn around, I see Jack come around from behind the bar, come to me and give me a great big hug and kiss. I was on cloud nine. I grabbed him again and started kissing him. He was yelling in my ear, "Hang on, easy, I have to get back behind the bar, Happy New Year!" I yelled in his ear, "You are coming over after work!" He nodded and said, "Check in later."

The rest of the night was just blurry at Chatter. I remember doing more shots, drinking more drinks and dancing my ass off with Jaime and Liza. We lost Robyn and Scott. No one really seemed to care. We were all taking cabs, everyone knew how to get home and all I knew was Jack was coming over. As this was all going on I texted Dennis.

ME*: Happy JHapyy New Year*

Oh God! Typical drunk text! The lights flipped on and everyone looked like holy hell! The bouncers were pushing everyone towards the door and we all had to get in line for the cabs and shuttles. The entire place was bat Shit crazy! I stole a piece of pizza right out of someone's pizza box. We were all falling all over each other! As we waited in the cab line, Robyn and Scott surfaced. Robyn's hair was a complete knotted mess and she had one eye half shut! This was a great night, but I still felt empty. No matter how drunk I was, I had my wits about me to keep remembering that I was a wife once and now I am in a bar. I had a little private pity party in my head which was probably the alcohol. All I knew was I needed to snap myself out of it and stay strong.

We loaded into our cab and poured back out of it at the house. I wanted everyone to stay awake in case Jack came back. I started to open beers and blast music. We were all awake, still dancing and some of our friends started filtering in. Scott invited people back to our place, so it turned into a great big after party. As I did an Alabama Slammer, at the kitchen table with five strange guests, Jack walked in. He was completely loaded. I ran over to him, dragged him in the kitchen, got him a beer and would not let him out of my sight.

Things went hazy and within a quick blink, I opened my eyes to beaming sunlight in my bedroom! I knew where I was but did NOT really. I knew someone was next to me. It was Jack and I had all my clothes on. I also had a random scrunchie on my wrist that was not even mine. I ignored that for a while and made my way to the kitchen. I literally had no recollection of anything since the Alabama Slammer. I remember Jack coming in the house, but I do not really remember how or when we ended up in my bed. And why do I have a scrunchie on my wrist? Did I put my hair up at some point? Oh no! Did I give him what he asked for the first time? That is the ONLY reason I would whip my hair up. OH MY GOD!

***

Note to self, always take the day after New Year's Day off, especially when you are three hours away from home. Everyone woke up with hangovers beyond belief! We cleaned, packed and got in the car in silence. No one talked about the night before, and no one remembered anything! We were all half laughing but too tired to figure out what to talk about.

Jaime asked me quietly in the backseat, what I was going to do with Jack. I said, "Nothing." What was I supposed to do? I do not even remember what happened. If I had to bet my life on it, I know exactly why there was a scrunchie around my wrist. I could not even THINK about it. I almost started to cry. I looked out the window and started to panic. I struggled about what I was doing, but at the same time wanted to allow myself to have fun. So why was I so hard on myself? There is more to this garbage thing then just men. It is mental, emotional, physical garbage whirling around in my head!

I was the first to get dropped off. I struggled down the driveway into the house because I was so tired. Gwen was on the couch all bright eyed and bushy tailed, "How was it?" I sat down, sighed and told her the whole story. She laughed the whole time. As I started to bring myself down and talk to her about why I might have been a bit sad or off, my phone rings. It was DENNIS!!!

I jumped up and started waving at Gwen to be quiet. All of a sudden there was severe pep in my step. I answered. "Hey, it's Dennis, I wanted to catch up with you because I fell asleep last night. Saw your texts. Sorry we did not ever hook up over the week." I said no problem, asked how he liked the mountain and totally did not let on that I was with Jack and a scrunchie in my bed. He asked me if I wanted to get together this week for a drink, since we are both in Connecticut. I said yes, and he said he would call me Thursday. Wow, that whole situation wrapped up nicely in a bow, not a scrunchie!

***

It was mid-week and the days were so painful after the fantastic holiday season and the Killington trip. I was so tired and still hung over, I could not even think of whether or not Dennis was really going to call me on Thursday. He did not even know me. Robyn said he was very nice and looked like the type of guy that did not play games. Well I hope so. I am about ready for something normal!

As I was driving home from work that Wednesday, I gave myself a lot of credit and patted myself on the back for being more positive than before and proud of living my life instead of defining it by a man. I knew I was having fun, not searching for a husband anymore, but I was still constantly lining up men. I am making progress, but I am still not quite there.

I get home and see my one staple every night. My Gwennie! Every night when I walk in the door she is sitting at the kitchen table with a glass of wine, a magazine and her legs are always crossed with her foot shaking back and forth, pulsating under the table. She was my rock, and I enjoyed coming home every night and having a friend to talk to.

Before she could get any words out I said, "Can we get take out, I'm starving and do not feel like cooking." She jumped up with the same idea. I guess I read her mind. She grabbed her coat, I already had mine on. We hopped back in my car and drove to the restaurant down the street. Yup there's Giovanni and Pajama Pants Paul, again. We always run into them at this restaurant. We went over to the bar to say hello. We gave each other Happy New Year kisses and walked over to the end of the bar to place a takeout order.

While we were waiting, I felt like being anti-social. Gwen went over to talk to the guys a bit more. I was just too cranky and hungry. When I grabbed the food that was ready, I walked over to the guys, said goodbye and dragged Gwen out. She kept saying, "I don't know why you don't like Paul, he is such a doll." I said, "I did like Paul and was attracted to him when we worked together but he freaked me out a little the night he came over. And I don't understand why he wears his pajama pants to work?" I complained to Gwen that when you admire someone from afar, they seem like they are just dreamy. Then, when you get to know them, the dream just dies! They are never at all what you dream they would be, and you wish you never ruined the fantasy. That is me with Pajama Pants Paul.

As we walk in the house my phone rings! It is Dennis, again! Oh my God! "Hello." Gwen is smirking and setting up our table for our feast. Dennis called to see if I still wanted to do a drink Thursday night. I said yes and asked him where he wanted to meet. He said, "I'm not making you drive out here, I will come out to you." WOW! What a nice guy. I do not think anyone has been generous and respectful like that to me in a very long time. I picked where I thought would be fun to go, that was quiet enough to talk, yet fun. He said he would look it up on the internet and meet me there at six thirty p.m. Thursday. That was tomorrow!!!!!

Gwen actually shrieked when I hung up my phone. We both were laughing and smiling. I got very nervous and told her I was scared because I did not know him. She said that was a good thing because I never step out of my comfort zone and always go after people I know or dated before. I agreed. We started to eat, and I made her talk all about herself and what is going on with her. I was exhausted by my life and wanted to focus on her!

Bedtime was early, and I was on pins and needles trying to fall asleep knowing I was going to see Dennis the next day. I woke up the next morning full of energy. Work was pretty uneventful in my software engineering world. When the clock struck five, I sprinted out the door. I wanted to run home, curl my hair, put more make up on and arrive at the restaurant as though I looked that great all day! I literally ran into the house, down the hall and did what I had to do, and then ran out! I got there at six thirty. As I was pulling up, he was right there waiting outside the door. I thought that was sweet because it was kind of cold out.

I walked up to him, kissed him on the cheek and we walked inside. He was even more gorgeous in Connecticut than he was in Vermont. He was dressed very stylish with these cool black Italian leather shoes. I was actually proud to walk in with him and hoped someone I knew saw me. We got a table. It was nice, he kept saying he wanted to talk and not be somewhere very noisy. The hostess sat us. And that was the last time I remember a smile on my face.

I realized quickly, when everyone is in Killington, everyone is in mountain mode. You talk about snowboarding or skiing to break the ice when you meet someone, and everyone seems to have that in common. Also, everyone looks gross after skiing and liquor is always involved. I did not recall his voice, personality or grammar being an issue in the Killington Base Lodge. I know the girls would have noticed too. We must have been dazed, tired and liquored up. I would not look up at him because I was uncomfortable, and this was just really out of my comfort zone to be with this stranger outside of Vermont! We started talking about food, what different restaurants we liked and how we try to eat healthy. I sort of felt something was off. No sooner does he pick his head up from the menu and says let's just order then I have to tell you something. I thought okay. Hmmm, this can go many ways but after my Bull Shit trash over the years, I reasoned with myself that whatever he had to say cannot be that bad.

We order, and he says, "I worked today so I could pay for dinner cuz I'm a real gentleman, so I'd never let you pay." I thought, *weird, he worked so he could pay?* Then he said alright there's something you need to know. I am in the middle of a nasty divorce. I said, "Ok we've all been there that's not a big deal." Now, he proceeds to completely bash his ex-wife and tell me the whole story. Hands are flying. Grammar is just horrible, and I was kind of staring blank and sucking back my drink with the cocktail stirrer straw and my head cocked to the right. I was a bit speechless. He was calling her a raging "c word." It was awful. So, I just replied "You clearly have some serious healing to do. You seem very hurt and not ready to date, don't you think?" He said, "Let me tell ya something, the next girl I meet is going to have a TON ah money and take care of ME for a change". Alrighty! I wanted to crawl under the table. I just wanted to leave! And as the night was going on, he was getting uglier and uglier and his grammar just sucked. So now the plates are clear, and the waiter asks if we want coffee or dessert. He says, "You got lattes like Starbucks?" I almost Fucking died. The waiter replied, "No just cappuccino, coffee or tea." He says, "Yea but no lattes or fancy *cawfee* like at Starbucks?" I jumped in and said, "There's a coffee shop next door, so let's just go there." He pulls out two wrinkled twenties out of his back pocket and says, "What am I supposed to do, I don't know how this works do I pay for the whole thing, I mean that's what I thought happens on a date?" I said, "Well you can pay or we can split it. Whatever works?" He said, "No I'll pay. I can't let a woman pay but I tell ya what, this dating is Bull Shit! I always have to pay on Saturday nights and then I don't like them. It's like opening my window and letting the cash fly out!" Again, making me feel really good and special. I was so disgusted I didn't even want to engage in what he was saying!

Next stop was the coffee house. He ordered an Oreo cookie latte, pretty fancy, and I ordered a vanilla nut tea. He stood away from the register and kept looking at the desserts while the barista said, "Twelve ninety-nine." I thought, *Hmm,*

I guess I am paying. I just took out my bank card and paid. He just expected it and I just figured let me pay and get the Fuck out of here. So, I walked outside with him and said, "Well, good luck with everything. I'm going to head home. Thank you for dinner." He nodded his head at me and said, "I'm never gonna hear from you again huh?" I said, "Well you don't seem like you are in a good place, but certainly, as a friend, keep in touch." I kissed him on the cheek and skyrocketed on over to my car. I was driving home thinking I am NEVER wasting a night on a guy I do not know, EVER AGAIN!!

When I got home, I got ready for bed and realized, I am okay without dating so much and always being on the lookout for a guy. Why am I so fixated on that? That was the worst night ever and I was pissed off! I figured I do have to meet people, but man the more garbage I take in the more I have to throw out!

Chapter 7

Several weeks had gone by and I had only had that one ridiculous date with Dennis. Life just sort of dragged on, but this weekend was going to be fun! I am excited for the mogul challenge coming up in Killington this Saturday. The mogul challenge is like the Yale/Harvard tailgate of Connecticut or the Army/Navy game of college football. Apparently, this mogul challenge is broadcasted on ESPN and is a big deal. Everyone tailgates along the side of the mountain and watches all of the competitions. I am definitely excited to go tomorrow! I am not rushing so much to get up to Vermont this particular Friday.

We rally in a commuter and head on up to Vermont. It was snowing a little bit, which is exciting to us! The three girls immediately asked me about my date with Dennis. Ugh! As I am explaining detail by detail they are screaming "What!!" And "No he DIDN'T," the whole time. I was half laughing, half disgusted and just tired. I told them I was DONE for a while and no one believed me.

We decided to stay in this Friday night. We were unpacking, laying out our Mogul Challenge outfits and I continued to nag about making sure the house is clean! I just do not understand. The lease is up in a few weekends and no one is concerned about cleaning but me! "Can you please shut the Fuck up about the cleaning?" Liza yelled up the stairs. "I want that security deposit back. No SHENNANIGANS this weekend!" I yelled.

I turned in pretty early after watching a few movies. Went into my bed and started "thinking" of course. Got to keep taking out that trash in my mental head or I swear it will pile up and weigh me down. I kept thinking in my head why everyone around me had it easy. All my friends back home were on second homes, second babies and I was still living the single life, paying my own bills, going to bars all the time and could not meet a good guy! Trust me, I am grateful for my life. My Killington girls are just as special to me, if not more than anyone back home but I wanted to be married and have a family! All my friends and family back home have this great life. I just always thought I would be a part of that and it makes me sad. This life is really Fucking tiring and I am getting fat from all the beer! I tossed and turned a bit trying to justify why I have been dealt this hand in life, why I pick one loser after the next, then I guess my mental trash piled up, tired me out and I fell asleep.

I woke up well rested. I ran up the stairs like it was Christmas day and presents were waiting for me under the tree. It was the day of the mogul challenge. I had been told about it from the first day on this mountain. People up here in Killington wait all year for this party! I got everyone out of bed and yelled "Be by the car in an hour!" Everyone hustled around and got ready to leave the house. First stop, a Bloody Mary at Killington base lodge. Everyone was there, we were having so much fun. First, I snuck in a quick nag, as I was momma of the house. I reminded them to go easy these next few weekends with inviting people over. We had to keep the house clean as the season was almost over. I want that security deposit back! Then, I was asking everyone if they got their ashes. This past Wednesday was Ash Wednesday and I was so crazed about getting my ashes, I kept texting and calling everyone. I felt I was sinning more so than usual and thought the literal ash cross on my forehead was going to mean I get to go to heaven or something. I had even stopped at a pizza place on the way back to my office after the ash service. The woman at the counter made a mistake and gave me a piece with sausage on it and I waved both my hands "Ooooh no, it's Ash Wednesday, I can't eat meat, I need all the help I can get!"

No sooner are we making small chit chat, does the entire base lodge fill up! You could not even move, and the mogul challenge was not starting for another hour. I looked over the top of the bar to the open windows that were floor to ceiling. The most insane view of the mountain with the flags out for the races were facing us, as well as all the party tents alongside of the mountain, as high as I can see them. Everyone was setting up their parties. Even one tent had an acoustic guitar player. This is SICK. So much more fun than being home. I mean what else would I be doing this particular Saturday at home, cleaning and watching the Hallmark Channel because all my friends would be at their kid's games!

We sucked down our Bloodies and walked outside. We decided to buy a wristband and "party hop" instead of setting up our own tent. This way we would not miss out on anyone else's fun all day. The drinks were flowing. It was so cold out, I kept sucking down my drinks to stay warm, not realizing we had a long day and night ahead of us still. There were so many people that I had never seen before! Jaime was hell bent on standing next to the guitar player, so we camped out over there for a while. We were sipping drinks, people watching and dancing a bit when no sooner do I get a tap on the shoulder from Jack. "Heyyyyy what's up," I said. I was a little bit nervous about the whole New Year's Eve and scrunchie incident still even, though so much time had passed. He hung out with us and kept standing behind me rubbing my back. Oh, good Lord! I love him, he is so adorable. When I get up the nerve, later, I am going to ask him what exactly happened on New Year's Eve.

He was all about hanging out with us. The girls liked him, not for me, but liked him. I do not understand why they do not like him for me? He has been pretty steady in the game since the beginning of the season, I know he is messed up a lot, but he is really nice and fun to be with. The girls always tell me when they see him talking to other girls, or "I heard this", "I heard that" but we are not dating, so technically he can be with whoever he wants. What am I supposed to do? Scott insists he is "casting" when he texts me at night. He thinks he puts the cast out there like a fisherman and sends as many texts to as many girls and see who "bites". That is ridiculous! I never heard of men doing that, although there have been times that he would text me "What's up?" at night and I would reply and say, "Want to hang out?" and I would never hear from him again. Was I one of those fish that did not BITE in time?

Anyway, he was with me now and I could care less about anything from the past. The end of the season was right around the corner and I just wanted to soak in all the fun, laughs and antics we had left for the year. Robyn and I went off to find a bathroom. We were standing in front of two gorgeous men in the Porto-let line and kept whispering so they couldn't hear, "I'd like to rip your neck gator off with my teeth," "I'd like to lick the icicle hanging off of your crotch right now." And just giggling and snuggling with each other to keep warm. No sooner does one of the men behind us say "How cute you two are. Mother, daughter?" We both turned around like the devil and his daughter, "YEA WHICH ONE OF US IS SUPPOSED TO BE THE MOTHER!" They both got so scared they did not answer. I said, "Yea you better turn around!" I wonder which one he thought was the daughter? That was so freaking embarrassing! But we were kind of old!

Robyn and I cackled the whole way back to the group, arguing "I think he thought you were the mother!" I was getting so tipsy but in a very silly way. We made it back over to everyone, and Jack was sitting on the plank that was holding up the make-shift stage that the guy playing the guitar was standing on. He pulled me into his lap. He was digging my dirt today! He was totally hammered but digging me! Everyone was just socializing like we were at a bar, but we were outside, standing in freezing snow! Not one person was paying attention to the actual races going on. It was just such a GREAT DAY. I finally got the nerve up to ask Jack about New Year's Eve. I said, "Oh my God I haven't really hung out with you this much since New Year's." Jack said, "Yea I was pretty banged up when I got to your house, but not half as bad as you guys were, it's all good though." I said, "I have to tell you I kind of don't remember falling asleep, last visual I had was everyone doing shots in the kitchen." He started laughing like Spicoli from Fast Times at Ridgemont High, I was like "What????" He said, "Dude you started throwing up in the bathroom. I had to take care of you, stand there and hold your hair back. Finally, I found an elastic thing under the sink and made you put your hair up, so I can go back out and party. Then later I crashed with you, you were passed out!" Nooooooo! I never fooled around with him!!??!! The scrunchie was because I was vomiting! I am such a LOSER! I have been killing myself all winter wondering about that Fucking scrunchie!!!!

"Oh, thank God!" I yelped. I explained to him how I thought that scrunchie meant I did something else that required me to keep my hair back. He laughed and said, "You into doing that tonight?" Part of me wanted to slap him, the other part of me was kind of smitten. I was not seeing that he was a booby prize that no one else wanted! And his comment was disrespectful not flirty!

As the party started dwindling down we moved immediately to Chatter. Chatter was hosting the "after party." We took a shuttle from the mountain. There were people and traffic EVERYWHERE. I never saw anything like it. I was feeling pretty good but totally holding my own. I kept yelling at Scott, "Don't you dare invite ANYONE back to the house tonight, we have to keep the place clean and free of damage for THREE MORE WEEKENDS!" Jaime and Liza kept breaking my balls "We are inviting the entire bar over!" I gave them one of my Mother Hen, knock it off looks, then the finger.

Chatter was awesome! Set up just like New Year's Eve in hopes of a crazy crowded night. I was psyched Jack was not working tonight so he stayed with us the entire time. We were all standing right in front of this great band. There were tons of wild people on the dance floor. Liza fell right into me and I fell onto the lead singer and tipped over one of their speakers. The singer was in mid song and said "Whoa, easy out there!" I yelled "Tell the crowd to stop pushing us!" The singer said "Hey, easy out there, you are trampling over my ladies up here in the front!" Meanwhile it was us the whole time, we just didn't want to singer to think we were obnoxious drunks!

So, as the night went on, I was thinking, we have no business still being at a bar right now after the long day we have had. Jack and I kept finding each other here and there as we would go off dancing, drinking, and socializing. The last time we found each other was when I had been searching everywhere for Liza and Robyn. I found Jaime and she was with some of her other friends who she ran into from Connecticut. I knew she would be okay and go back to wherever they were staying. I hoped that Liza and Robyn had each other, and Scott usually fends for himself, hoping to pick up a girl. I yelled in Jack's ear, "I can't find anyone, but I think I want to go home." He said, "I'll go with you, I'm beat." When we were in the cab line, I realized I did not have keys with me. I told Jack and he said it was "no biggie" we'd just go back to his house. *Nice*, I thought.

Jack and I pulled up to his house and I offered to pay for the cab, but he insisted on paying. Again, nice little checkmark, in favor of the pill popping klutz! We go into his house and go into his room. None of his housemates were home yet, but it was that long of a day that there were no beers being cracked open for after hours. We talked for a bit, he gave me some sweats and got in bed. I thought to myself, *Oh no! He probably thinks I am going to put my hair in a scrunchie and go down on him, since he proposed that idea this afternoon.* Well, I was the one who put it in his head, no pun intended! I rolled over towards the wall and pretended to sleep. He kept hugging and spooning but I got off easy, he must have been so wrecked he passed out. Phew!

The next morning, we talked a bit about some funny stuff that happened the day before and he asked me if I ever found out where Liza and Robyn were. I had never heard from them, checked my phone and said, "I'm sure they are fine." We rounded up our things and he offered to take me home. As we were driving, I thought I could see myself with Jack, but kept thinking, what are you doing? Is there not a normal guy out there, that maybe wants to date exclusively, instead of hooking up? Or possibly a non-pill popper this time since, I left my own marriage because of something just like that! I was too tired to think this through, I just wanted to get home and get on my own couch. As we pulled up the, house looked fairly quiet. It looked to me like all was good!

I give Jack a kiss goodbye and told him to check in during the week. Told him I would see him soon. I walk up the front walk and stand at the front porch ready to knock. I see Scott in the kitchen window. He very quietly murmurs, "Hi mamma!" "Hi Scott," I say with a cute little smile. All of a sudden, I realize, he is speaking to me through the kitchen window only there is no window! It was like a takeout window situation at a drive thru. My face turned cold and I said, "Why the Fuck am I talking to you through NO WINDOW?" He said, "We had a little accident." I yelped "WHAT?" Mind you I am still standing outside on the porch because I had no key. He said, "It's a long story come in." I squawked, "UNLOCK the door, or should I jump in through the window frame!" Scott opened the door, I walked in the door like a complete lunatic! All I kept saying in my head was, *we broke a Fucking window RIGHT before the lease ends and I am not paying for it, I was not home.* I walk into the living room. Liza is sitting on the loveseat and Robyn is laying on the couch in a hand cast and sling. I said, with a very mean condescending tone, "What is going on right now?!"

Robyn was shaking and quivering, and here is how it went down:

Robyn: "I cut my hand on the glass."

Ella: "What glass?"

Robyn: "The kitchen window."

Ella: "Why was the kitchen window the reason you cut your hand? Not catchin what you're throwin!"

Robyn: "Well Liza and I took a cab home early, we couldn't find you. We were looking for our keys and couldn't find them. So, I picked up the shovel on the front porch and smashed the kitchen window."

Liza: "I was crying because I was so cold, and I lost my jacket!"

Robyn: "After I smashed the glass, I hoisted myself up on the back of the milk crate out there and I slipped. The glass just sliced my hand. Ella there was blood everywhere!"

Scott: "So I got scared because I heard the smash and when I opened the door Robyn was bleeding really bad. We called 911!"

Ella: "Wait, wait STOP…what do you mean you heard the smash and opened the door?"

Scott: "Well I was home the whole time."

Ella: "You were HOME? DID YOU TWO IDIOTS BOTHER TO KNOCK OR RING THE DOORBELL BEFORE YOU THREW A SHOVEL INTO THE KITCHEN

WINDOW? THAT WAS YOUR FIRST AND BEST IDEA TO GET THE DOOR OPEN?????"

Robyn: "I know I'm so sorry, we just were so cold we were confused!"

Ella: "THE SEASON IS OVER.... what are we going to do about this??"

Robyn: "Well, do you want to hear what happened with my hand!?"

I felt really bad, realizing I did not ask if she was ok or be optimistic and say, "It could have been worse." So, I threw myself down onto the couch and sighed, "What else happened?" Robyn and Liza proceeded to tell me how the paramedics came, Liza went running downstairs to put a sweatshirt on because she thought she could go in the ambulance, she tripped over shoes on the stairs and went tumbling down. Then the paramedics explained that Liza was not family and she could not ride in the ambulance. The paramedics took Robyn away, she got stitches and had to take a cab home today for thirty dollars! Cannot make this Shit up!

When everyone calmed down we decided we would try to take care of the window ourselves and not tell our landlord. I started making coffee. Went to the kitchen and squawked, "You're lucky it's nice out! There's no Fucking window, in the kitchen, in Vermont." Just took me a little time to let it go. We started talking about where I was during all this. I sat down and told them in detail my night with Jack. I told them NOTHING happened on New Year's with the scrunchie. I told them that Jack explained that my hair was up from full on vomiting. Again, nice visual, cannot make this Shit up.

We figured it was time to start packing up to leave. We had a big day yesterday and no one wanted to leave Robyn alone to go snowboard. While we were packing, we left Robyn like a limp injured bird on the sofa and packed all her bags. I kept talking about how awesome Jack was with me. I sort of grazed over the fact that he was totally under the influence of something, but it was fun!

After a long ride with tons of traffic, we got our cars at the commuter lot. I drove home slowly. As I pulled into the driveway, I noticed Gwen had taken the trash out. I looked at that pile of garbage bags and knew I should throw Jack out, but I was just not ready. I snuck in quietly passed Gwen's closed bedroom door and flopped on my bed. I noticed a voice mail on my phone. Hmmm, I do not remember it ringing. And do not remember seeing the notice that I had a message! I logged in and pressed 1 for play.

"Yeah Ella, Fuck you Ella, you leave me at a bar cuz you think you are too cool to hang out with me. Let me tell ya something, I'm cooler than your friends, I'll mess them up. You're not gonna hang out with me cuz your Fuckin friends think I'm a punk. Fuck you. You're a loser......" I had NO IDEA who it was and NO RECOLLECTION of his voice!

The next day I got to work, texted and emailed everyone half cracking up and half nervous from this belligerent stranger on my voicemail. I made them listen to the message. I forwarded it to Liza, emailed it to Robyn and Jaime and then made Scott listen at lunch.

Some of my innocent co-workers were in shock. "Who on earth would leave a voicemail like that?" I said "That's what's out there!! This is my inventory when I go out, spanning from Connecticut to Vermont, they suck!" My really nice admin said "No actually it's not what's out there. It's what you are choosing to do, where you are choosing to go and who you are choosing to mingle with!" Oh my God, I thought that hundreds of times myself but to hear it from someone on the outside hurt! I felt like I got hit over the head with a two by four!

I was so disgusted when I left work, I decided to go to the mall. I just felt beat up. Life could be so amazing one hour and so crazy stressful the next hour. Gwen was calling me about eating, my mother was calling to see if I had something to eat for supper like I am twelve. I just wanted to be alone.

I started to walk around in the mall. I got so tired that I did not feel like buying anything or trying anything on. I was just walking around like a complete fool. I went by the chair massages and the row of chairs were glowing and I could swear I heard Angels!! Just what the doctor ordered! I get in the line and one of the Asian massage men starts waving me and another girl to go with him. "I give you massage on table." He takes us over to their store front. It was completely legit and clean. "Five extra dollar, I do massage on table, five extra dollar!" Okay cool. Worked for me. I hop on the massage table in the middle of a row of people getting massaged. My little Asian man starts at the shoulders. "UH GOOD LORD!" It felt sooooooo good. I was so relaxed and sinking in to the comfortable table. I was starting to dream a bit. I was imagining who I might end up with this year. Was it Jack? I wonder if Pajama Pants Paul amounts to something when ski season is over. Then I thought about the window.

My face was in the hole at the edge of the table, arms by my side, palms up. All of a sudden, the massage guy leans all the way over to get his hands on my far shoulder from where he was standing and completely cups his balls in my palm. My eyes immediately opened wide. I am whispering in my head, *"Oh my God, Oh my God, his balls are in my hand!"* Now I start laughing, I try not to move because I do not want him to think I like the balls in my hand, but I am trying to get them OUT of my hand. No sooner does he move around the other side of the table. I clench my hands together in two little fists, so it does not happen again, and I just get up, pay and walk out. I was laughing so hard in the car all by myself, I could not believe what happened. Why are there always stories with me? Why?

On my way home, my father calls me, "Yea, Ella, we are all going to the casino this weekend with Liza and Jaime's parents. Do you girls want to meet us, I can get you a room?" I squealed, "OMG YES! I will tell them, and we can meet you there Saturday around 6pm. We are just going up Friday night to finish packing on Saturday and can shoot over to the casino on the way home! Thanks DAD!" My dad mumbled, "Alright, call me Saturday when you are close." Then there was dead silence, he never says goodbye, he just hangs up.

I sold the girls on the casino! That Friday was our final ride of the year up to Killington Mountain. I have to say I was depressed. I loved leaving Connecticut and my trash behind, but I realized I was starting let some Killington trash pile up higher than the highest mountain top! It was starting to wear on me! I never saw George again, we were two ships passing on I-91 and Scott was going to fix the window and finish closing up the house on Sunday.

We rolled into the house Friday evening and plopped on the couches. Liza decided it was necessary to go to The Barn and Chatter one last time, get up very early and pack up the house. I was sure I needed to see Jack before I left. I figured I would just text him because he was working and go to his place really quick to say so long, not goodbye.

The Barn was like a ghost town. No one was there. We had a drink and when to Chatter. At this point, I felt like everyone who had houses in Killington were just burnt out! We walked over to the bar that Jack was tending at. He was so disheveled for some reason. Not the usual hot looking Jack. "Here she isssssss!" He was so out in left field tonight. Who the hell knows what he was "on" but I did not even care and just said, "Hi! I just wanted to come say bye because we are leaving tomorrow morning. But you have my number, so let's definitely get together over the Spring. He said, "Yea absolutely, my buddies and I are going to Utah for two weeks, then when I get back I'll give you a shout." He turned to everyone else and nodded, "Bye ladies!" We all waved, smiled and walked away. For some reason, I was just "tired." Did not care, one way or another, that I was saying "So long!"

Chapter 9

What a way to wrap up the winter and head into spring. We cleaned everything we could clean at the house, said goodbye to Scott and were actually ready to wrap up winter. I took a look at the house, as I was stepping into the front seat of the truck and really felt grateful for the opportunity to spend time up there this winter. Now we are headed to the casino in the woods!

We are eagerly awaiting the exit to the casino and still in just as good of a mood as we were when we were heading to Killington six months ago. I learned a lot up there about what I want and what I deserve, and this is the first time I really want to just be with the girls instead of looking for a guy tonight. I think I may be ready to stop taking in garbage. "Next exit!" Liza yells, as we pass the sign for the exit.

I was looking forward to not being cold for a change. We pull up to the valet and spill out of the truck. Naturally, the valet guy was hot and we all started flirting with him and acting stupid. We were meeting my family at check in and going to our rooms. We just wanted to unload our bags and roll on over to any bar for late afternoon Bloody Mary's. At the lobby fountain stood my parents, Liza's mom and my nieces and nephews. We all hugged as if we had not seen each other in five years, yet I saw them all three days ago.

My dad held up the two key cards. As I reached for the two key cards, he lifted them up with a bent elbow squawking "Now this room is not near our room, you girls better behave and take it easy tonight, you have been partying and drinking all winter." I said, "Dad I'm not twelve, we are fine! Just go have fun with the kids we will check in later!"

We all part ways and go to our rooms, not to meet up again until after dinner. As soon as we got to the room we freshened up, unloaded some alcohol we took with us from the house and started playing music. Jaime was laying out all her shirts asking what she should wear at night. For some reason, I had a funny feeling we were going to be having too much fun, right away, to go back and shower again.

Robyn and Liza were antsy for a Bloody Mary, so I freshened up, did my makeup, brushed my teeth, just in case we were never coming back. We looked decent but not for dinner and casino night clubs. We went to the first bar, plopped right in the middle of the casino, and the Bloody Mary's were flowing. I kept getting texts from Jack-

Hey what are you up too?

I didn't answer.

Hey, let me know if you want to stop over for drinks before my shift.

Ummmm did he not remember I was LEAVING? Mind boggling. He probably has no clue, again, that we talked which means he has no recollection of me telling him I was leaving. But I still had that little bit of garbage piling back up in the back of my head, intrigued that he wanted to see me. *No Ella he does not want to see you, he is casting the net for anyone who might want to hook up before his bar shifts. Snap out of it,* I thought. Well at least I am aware this time!

When I came back from my brief fog of texting with Jack and my dumb day dreaming, I realized we were all really buzzed at a bar in the middle of the casino. Liza's phone rings, she mouths to me, our moms want us to meet them at the stores because my mom wants to buy me a purse. We thought that was a tremendous idea! Let's go shopping. It was only four thirty pm. We were very silly and wobbling through the crowd over to the drag of stores and food court. We were just strolling around and window shopping while we were waiting for our moms.

We walked into this pretty boutique. Robyn went off looking for clothes and the rest of us crowded around the counter with the bags. In walked our mothers. They did not notice our buzz. Liza's mom points to the bag and Liza said "Ew that's gross!" Her mom scowled and said alright then is there anything else you see that you like. We started browsing around the store. I was in need of keeping the buzz going. I said if we find anything we like we will let you know and come back after breakfast tomorrow. "Perfect!" Jaime yelled. Her parents were not at the casino yet, and she did not want to run into them in her silly state. Jaime's mom, Auntie Michelle, has no problem pulling her hair or cracking her if she is not behaving. Mind you we are ADULTS! And mind you we are never behaving. We separated from the moms and went back to the store to get Robyn. As I lurked under the dressing room stalls to see where Robyn was, I see Liza coming at me with a mannequin hand. My eyes widened I said, "What is that?" She said, "It was just sitting on the floor in the corner." She looked right, left and smoothly slipped it in her purse, like we did the drum sticks and everything else we thought we were entitled to have, that wasn't ours. I just looked straight and ran away from her. I was laughing, wobbling and scurrying out the door. I landed on a bench in front of the store. Liza and Jaime came out after me and we were just camped out waiting for Robyn.

Low and behold, the hand comes out. Liza has it on her cheek as if she is pondering a thought. I am snapping pictures. Jaime is grabbing it and walking behind people pretending to grab their ass, as I am taking more pictures. It was a sideshow. We were crying laughing but everyone else was sort of just staring. They did not think it was as funny as we did.

Next stop was a Mexican restaurant for apps and Margaritas. No sooner do I order, DING.... It's Jack-

Yea lemme know if u wanna stop by before my shift within the next hour.

I thought, *are you kidding me! I was with you last night and told you I was leaving. We said goodbye!!! Do you even Fucking remember???*

DING...
I wanna see you with your shirt off

I was a raging lunatic. How dare he speak to me that way!!! I have a right to be mad. I talked to him this whole winter, he never remembered stuff and always hung out with me when he was annihilated. I was completely disgusted. I wrote back-

Listen, I'm not going to be around anymore so take care and good luck...you're an idiot!

He replied-

fuck you!!

"Haaaaaaaaa" I actually started laughing. He really expressed himself with the two exclamation points! I shared the text with the girls. We all started having a ball making fun of him, his grammar, and anything else we could find ridiculous about him!
I just kept sucking down my Margaritas. The hand joined us in the center of the table, it was our pet "Thing".

Groggy as all Fuck, I wake up at 6am and find myself in the chair by the window in our hotel room. Everyone was there, decent, no hook ups! I check for my phone and my wallet. All good. Then as I am brushing my teeth, I got a hit of alcohol anxiety. The night was fuzzy. We were bar hopping, dancing, "Thing" was with us, I never gambled, and I vaguely recall walking to the room with Liza.

I got a text from my family saying they were all going to breakfast at eight o'clock. I replied back that I was definitely not making it.

Everyone was asleep, and I just slipped over the chair and shut my eyes. I could not sleep. My mind raced, and my heart raced. I started to cry. I hated the way I felt. How can I have such a great time and wake up feeling so bad about myself the next morning? I was trying to think it through. I was not with anyone, we did not do anything wrong but have cocktails and laugh all night. What was missing? While the girls continued to sleep, I cleaned around the hotel room and put all of the garbage from my purse in the trash.

***

Everyone, including "Thing" made it back to New Haven with headaches and body pain. This was a crazy six months. Went out with a bang but I think I am ready to rest and refocus. I feel rejuvenated as I will throw out Jack with the garbage this week. My next hope is to stay focused, letting the good in and not the garbage!

Gwen and I had a nice Sunday cleaning and getting ready for Spring again. We had a lot of laughs this winter and could not wait for Summer! We were dusting, scrubbing floors and doing laundry. Later on, were sitting at the kitchen table when my phone rings. It is my dad! *Hmmm oh Shit, something is wrong I can sense it*, I thought. "Hello". "Yea we got a problem!" *Oh Shit*, my life flashed before my eyes. *What did I do? Where did I go? Who called and ratted me out?* I timidly reply, "What?"

Now my dad starts screaming, "My casino guy called me, you guys stole a haaaaannnd!" *Oh Noooooooooooo! I'm dead!* I thought. My dad, angry as all hell, continued, "Security has you four, on camera, with a hand all over the casino. The store wants this hand back or I'm getting in trouble and you are getting arrested and have to pay twenty-five hundred dollars for a new mannequin!!! You are an ADULT, I trusted you with the room, four ADULTS and this is the call I get!" I said, "Dad, it's not like they found cocaine in the room or something really bad!" He said, "I almost WISH it was! How do I explain that my grown daughter stole a mannequin haaaaaaaaand! Get me that hand tonight, I have to bring it up to the casino and return it!" I offered to return it for him, he said he was so embarrassed, he could not even think straight and needed to do it himself.

I am now completely psycho, calling Liza asking if she still has the hand. I caught her on a very stressful night working overtime at her job. She answered the phone, I said "Liza please tell me you still have the hand! We are in trouble with the casino and we are going to get fined twenty-five hundred dollars and possibly get arrested if the store presses charges!" She said, "I am not in the mood for jokes right now, please tell me you are kidding me, then I need to hang up!" I said, "I am NOT kidding, this is serious, my dad is so mad at us!" She sighed and said, "I will put the Fucking hand in a bag on my front porch when I get home tonight, pick it up in the morning!"

I called my dad, told him I was retrieving the hand by seven o'clock a.m. and would bring it over to him, "hand" delivered. I hung up the phone and looked at Gwen. She was completely entertained by all of this and just replied, "You guys are nuts!" As we got up from the table and continued to clean.

I turned my iPod on and got a bit silent while we were cleaning. I sort of felt like a loser. I kept hearing my Dad in my head, *you are an ADULT, I trusted you with the room, four ADULTS.* I had every intention of regrouping and refocusing before my father called. I knew I was not acting right. Am I a complete loser? I feel like I need to grow up, but I don't want to! What is WRONG with me? Maybe nothing is wrong with me and I am just falling victim to the guilt everyone else puts on me for trying to live my life. I have to sort through all of this.

Gwen and I finished cleaning and plopped ourselves down on the couch before bed for one last gab session. Gwen was smirking and shaking her head. I said "What!?" She said, "You girls are just too much." I said, "I know we try to have fun, but then we always push it to another level." Then I started to cry! Gwen was so cute, she sat up straight and yelped, "Are you CRYING?" I was just shaking my head. "I just don't want to do this anymore." "Do what?", Gwen asked. I could not get the syllables out, I was just in a hyperventilating cry. "This, eh, being, eh, alone." Gwen looked completely disgusted at me and said, "How are you ALONE, Ella?" I syllable breathed, "You, eh, know, eh, single. I hate, eh, being single. I want to be home, eh, with someone, eh, I'm tired."

Gwen moved closer to me on the couch, I was slouched over the far edge. "You have to stop! You are so fixated on being ALONE, I don't even know what that means. I enjoy my life, my friends, the guys I date, my job, I never feel alone. You had a fun winter that I would have loved to do with you if I had the money. You have a huge family and all of your friends have been your friends since you were six years old! I do not see why you are so sad. Is it because of a GUY?" I lifted my head. I stared at her but did not say anything. She was right, and I AM A LOSER. Why the Fuck am I crying over this fantastic life I have? I should feel full and satisfied with my family, my friends, my job and the great life I am lucky to lead. I just let the flood gates open. Started sobbing on her and hugging, saying, "You are right eh eh eh EH". When the crying stopped, I started laughing and wiping my face. Sat up and said "I am such a complete DOPE! I guess I am just tired, and my father yelling at me was just the icing on the cake. I need to go to bed. I think I just need to get back into a routine this Spring and just BE." She said, "Yes you are being ridiculous, stop CRYING!" Gwen was so disgusted with me! But in a good way, like a sister, I could count on her for the truth because she loves me. And we can laugh about it. I mean I always am fully aware that I am an idiot when it comes to this part of my life, but to hear it from someone else really puts it into perspective. I got up, got some water and got ready for bed.

After the washing of the face, brushing of the teeth and other routine bedtime stuff, I crawled into my clean sheets and just put the TV on. I was not paying attention though, I just was staring blank at the picture. The volume was not even up. *Get it together, what do you want, Ella?* I just kept thinking and was trying SO hard to come up with a plan. Maybe there was no plan. I know this needs to stop and I need to get this mental trash out of my head, but I just do not know how to do it!

The next morning, I felt very refreshed, I was very rested, which makes me more focused. The sun was shining into my bedroom and I was actually chipper. I went to the kitchen to make my coffee and get ready for work. This was the Monday I will look forward, get ready for a new season and be grateful for the fantastic winter I had in Killington. "Oh FUCK!", I yelled out loud and scurried, slipping and sliding in my socks down to my bedroom. "The HAND!" I had to deal with the Fucking hand. Now I had to rush and hurry up to get ready, so I can go to Liza's, get the hand on her doorstep, drive it to my dad's and then go to work. NEVER a dull moment. I am rushing around getting ready, never made coffee, pulled out something ridiculous from my closet and flew out the door. My mind was racing all the way to Liza's. My father is going to KILL me. I feel so bad, we are so immature.

I peel up to Liza's front door, fly out of the car, get the hand and run it to my parent's house. Thank God they go to work at like seven o'clock in the morning, so I was not going to see them face to face. I called my father and got his voicemail. "Dad, I put the hand in a grocery bag by your garage door. Thanks! Bye!" Pheww! Dodged that confrontation, retrieved the hand and "hand" delivered it. Off to work I go.

By the time I got to work, my father was already blowing up my phone. I answered, "Hello." My Dad was on the other end, "Ella, yea I'm going to the casino right now to deliver the hand." I said, "Dad, why did you leave work to deliver a HAND, this is stupid!" He said, "It's not stupid, they were going to arrest you and the guy I know convinced them not to, as long as we returned the hand! I'm telling you right now, I'm FED UP!" I said quietly, "Dad, ok, we are sorry, it was just innocent fun." He yelled, "Yea well, I want this CRAP to stop, GROW UP!" I replied like a pathetic five-year-old, who just got sent to her room, "I'm sorry Dad."

Not for nothing, but no one understands my life. I am single. What has to stop? A bunch of girls had a random night of fun, we did not commit a felony, we stole a limb from a mannequin! My Lord! I am so sick of everything and everyone today and it is not even nine o'clock in the morning yet!

Chapter 10

It is a beautiful Saturday and it is starting to look like Spring. I do not really think I ever realized how lucky I have it at this beach house. The house may be very close to the neighbors, ergo, when I see Giovanni, next door wooing a young lady. I can usually smell the candles and taste the parmesan right from my living room. So very close that my neighbor, to the left, usually catches me singing and dancing while vacuuming and then scurries away from the window when I catch his eye, pretending he did not just see me sliding and gliding to my Rick Springfield playlist. However, with that comes three hundred and sixty-degree views of the Ocean, stretches of beach on the Long Island Sound and the most beautiful views of the sky meeting the water like I have never seen before.

Gwen and I have this long, wrap around deck and spend any chance we get sitting outside with coffee, starting in the early weeks of Spring. This Spring is going to be different. I am grateful for the incredible winter I had in Killington but also am thankful for the Spring cleaning of the garbage I collected.

I will not take back any of the fun or the antics from this winter because I do believe that there is nothing, in life, better than laughing and we did quite a bit if that this past season on the slopes. But I do not feel the choices I made with guys were any better for me and I need to figure out what the Fuck I'm doing wrong! Well, I know what I am doing wrong, I just cannot seem to step out of the moment, every time there is a man in front of me and breathe for two minutes.

As I am sitting on the deck with my coffee, waiting for Gwen to get up, I went over some of the garbage I took in this winter. For instance, Jack. Jack was a pill swallowing, high, drunk, self-centered buffoon and yet I continued to park myself at Chatter for most of the winter months, when there could have been some really nice guys to talk to right near my barstool. Instead, I kept going back for the one person that showed me attention. Just because they show me attention does not mean I should give it back. I should be the one to decide and be a bit pickier and I am not! That's the problem!

I hear the swoosh of the slider opening and out walks Gwen with her coffee and blanket wrapped around her body. It is a gorgeous Saturday and we are deciding whether or not to perform our weekend cleaning or bag it and go hiking or the gym. As we banter basically about nothing, I decide we are going hiking. I have never been hiking but it seems like something I need to do to shed the beer gut I got at Chatter and The Barn this winter.

Gwen snapped, "Since when are you so into fitness, you want to just go for a walk? Hiking sounds a bit much let's ease into our Spring and Summer routine." Fine! I got up and put my sweats on and waited for Gwen to freshen up and get ready for our stroll through Cosey Beach. We rounded out of our driveway and headed toward the more populated area of the neighborhood. The restaurants were not showing any signs of life, as it was still early morning.

But the residents were biking, jogging and walking their dogs to and from their houses, to our town beach. This walk is showing me signs of a great season ahead of us. However, I am fat, white and need a tan, so I got me some work to do before that bathing suit comes on. As we are walking down the road, Gwen starts asking me about the fit I threw when I got in trouble with my dad last Sunday and the hand debacle. I sort of laughed but just explained that I was tired of all of it. Tired of the single life, the bars, getting into trouble, etc. "That has nothing to do with the fact that you stole a hand!" She yelled. "There were thousands of adults gambling, drinking and walking in and out of bars that night. Did they all have plastic mannequin limbs in their hands!? You guys are single yes, but you have to tone it down. I am not saying don't have fun, I love that you girls have a ball, I'm just saying you act like every weekend is Spring-break and it gets old!" She was so right. I could not even argue with her, I just looked at her with this shrewd look like *you are Fucking on to something!* I just did not realize it. I think the overcompensation of drinking and fun might be to mask the fact that we are alone and sort of "sad" on the weekends. And the viscous cycle continues because if we did not act like that, perhaps we would not be alone, as normal men would actually find us attractive.

We walked to the end of the pier near the town beach and pivoted around to head home. Literally, as I turn around I see Pajama Pants Paul on his bike riding towards our house, or really Giovanni's. He obviously did not have pajama pants on because I was kind of digging his frame from down the street. Just far away enough to see some buff. Before I can open my mouth, Gwen barked, "Look there's Paul, he was a nice guy and you did not want to talk to him anymore because he wore pajama pants to work! But you wasted all winter on that dick from Killington and the Fucking twin." I was so flustered and laughing I said, "I don't think ANY of them were all that! All three of them, including PJ Paul. What the hell am I supposed to do, there is no one out there." She said, "Let's just stop trying so hard and just let the summer unfold. It is still cold out, so let's focus on ourselves, get fit, get tan and let them find us!" She was right! I was all in. We walked briskly back to the house and cleaned the crap out of our rooms, the kitchen and scrubbed the crap out of the floors! The garbage is definitely going OUT today!

After our cleaning, I decided to go join the gym. This is probably my tenth gym membership in the past ten years because I get on a kick, join a gym, taking advantage of their monthly billing, go twice and then make a nice donation to their facility for the rest of the year. But, we will try this again. I want to get fit, trim, happy and enjoy the Summer.

I walk into the local gym franchise in town and walk up to the desk. "Hello, I'd like to join please." With a smile, this really fit young girl asks me to fill out all the forms and says, "You can sit right over there, ma'am." Ok that sucked, she "Ma'am'd" me! I sit down and fill everything out, get out my checkbook, license, etc. She sits with me and goes over all the policies, stands up and shakes my hand. I told her I would not be working out today because I already went for a walk. I just wanted to join and make sure I was ready to start coming in after work.

As I am walking out, I run into a very old friend from when I used to be married. We both locked eyes and knew we knew each other. He said "Ella?" I replied, "Yes! I wasn't sure if you recognized me, how are you?" His name was Dave, and he was an old friend of my ex-husband's. They had played softball together and we used to all go to games, drink afterwards and do fun stuff together when we were in our early twenties. I did NOT want to bring up my ex-husband, Chuck, and noticed he did not either. We were talking small talk, he said he had gotten married a few years back, but it did not work out. I told him I have not really found anyone worth talking about since I was divorced. He said he had not talked to any of those "softball" guys anymore. Davey was definitely dropping hints that he is single, he doesn't talk to "anyone" anymore, to me means he definitely is not friends with Chuck anymore. I was definitely feeling some vibes. No sooner does he say, "Well let's meet up for a drink sometime." I said "Definitely, how do I get in touch with you?" He whipped out his phone, so I shuffled in my bag for mine. We exchanged numbers, kissed each other goodbye, on the cheek, and parted ways.

I got in the car and felt really good. Thought to myself, *wow I just ran into an old friend, he wants to catch up, what a pleasant surprise.* I was thinking back to when I knew Dave and was trying to remember who he was. He was very tall and cute, but what else could I remember about him. *Oh yes,* I thought, *he is a plumber, lived with his mom back in his early twenties and was just really really polite and funny to all the softball wives.* I remember Dave just being a good guy. Nothing over the top exciting, but just a good guy. Well, we shall see what happens.

I pull up into my driveway and just cannot stop smiling. This Saturday has been such a gorgeous early Spring day. The late afternoon sun over the ocean was breathtaking and a nice bright change from the winter months in Killington. I walked up to my porch and noticed Gwen sitting on the patio. She turned her head, "Hey girl, how was the gym?" I said, "Oh I didn't work out I just joined." She smirked and giggled, "You're unbelievable." "What? Going to join the gym was a big motivational achievement for me! I walked in the morning for God sakes!", I yelled!

It is late afternoon and neither of us have plans for this lovely Saturday night. We were not really talking, just enjoying the sound of the ocean. Gwen blurts out with another smirk, "I have a date tonight." I jumped out of my seat, "You do? With who? Awesome!" She said, "This guy that my friend, from work, fixed me up with, we are going out for drinks early. I will be around later to meet up with you somewhere, it will not be all night with this guy." I was excited for her, but she was not very excited. I figured I would putz around and see what the girls were doing and meet up with Gwen at some point. I said, "Very cool, sounds like a plan." I got up and went inside and into my bedroom. As I turned the TV on and planned to rest for the last part of the afternoon, my cell phone rang. It was a number I knew looked familiar but spaced on who it could be. "Hello." "Hi, it's Dave, what's up?" His voice sounded deeper than at the gym and almost like he was trying to be cool. I said, "Oh my God, hey, how are you?" He said, "Good, I just finished working out and wanted to know if you wanted to grab a drink and some food tonight?" I replied, "Yea, I can probably do that." I did not want him to think I had NO PLANS. So, I acted like I can probably make that happen.

He asked if I could meet up with him at seven o'clock in downtown New Haven. He asked if I was in the mood for pizza and I said sure. We decided to meet at Pepe's Pizza, in New Haven. I am glad, it's casual, I have not been there in a while. We can have some beers, relax and catch up on life. I very quietly laid on my bed and took a nice relaxing nap.

Chapter 11

Here we go, I am all dolled up and heading to New Haven to meet up with Dave. I Fucking hate this! I just want to be in a normal relationship without putting on a show, going out with half-baked strangers, it is just getting old. But, at least I am out and taking a bite out of life. I cannot be in my house on a Saturday night, at this age, thinking everything I want is going to fall in my lap. *I have to work at this*, I thought.

I also thought to myself, *this might not be a date.* He asked me to meet him. This might just be two single people looking to rekindle a friendship. Who knows? I parked the car and walked down the street of our New Haven's own Little Italy section, of Wooster Street. I felt very safe and comfortable in this part of town, so I was fine meeting up with Dave, alone. Naturally, there was a line out the door of eager pizza eaters, waiting to get in to sample the number one pizza place in America! I saw from afar, Dave was already sort of in line and waving. I waved back, shuffled quickly up to him in the line and gave him a great big hug.

We immediately reconnected. Luckily, we had a lot of history and a lot of old friends to talk about, to keep our conversation going, until we were ready to be seated. When we sat down in a nice cozy booth, we immediately ordered a pitcher of beer. I was very relaxed, he was very sweet and very cute! I was really happy we did not bring up Chuck, and I assumed it was such old news, he had already heard what happened to us and what a train wreck Chuck was, so I did not even bother to rehash it.

I was really embarrassed for some reason and started to get an anxious stomach. You know when you are in a situation that you just want OUT? This man did nothing wrong, I just all of a sudden, did not want to be there anymore. I started breaking into a full-blown sweat and trying really casually to wipe the sweat rushing out of my pores. My entire face was wet as if I just ran a road race! It was so noticeable. I do not even know why it was happening. I could not stop it, to the point that I was sort of trying not to laugh. He was in the middle of a sentence. His sentence slowed down a bit as he cocked his head to the side and snickered, "Ella, are you ok? Do you need to go outside?" I said, "Oooh no I'm fine, it must have been the crushed red pepper." He kind of raised his eyebrows and scrunched up his nose and said hesitantly "Ohhh-kay." I was Fucking horrified. I was sweating, as if I just ran through a sprinkler in my backyard!

I managed to bring myself back to a normal state of cool, as far as my body temperature that is. I was so damn embarrassed at this point, I just wanted to go home. But he paid the bill and we went for a nice walk toward a nice area with a church, on a small-town green, in this quaint section of New Haven. We were sitting on the bench continuing our talk about some old mutual friends. We were gossiping about some blasts from the past: who got divorced, who slept with whose husband, and on and on. All of a sudden, I look him square in the face and now HE is beat red! I sort of laughed right in his face and said, "Oh my God, Dave are you okay?" He said, "Ella, I am so sorry, but I think if have to go, I can't breathe, and I think I am allergic to these flowers!" We were sitting under a Cherry Blossom Tree. This Cherry Blossom tree was gorgeous, and the trees were planted all over the town green. It was so beautiful, which was why we chose this bench to sit down in the first place!

Dave, literally, was lobster red in the face and was taking very short, wheezing breaths. We both stood up and walked very quickly to the car. He was walking in such a stride, I was almost running alongside of him to keep up. I had my head down and was thinking, *please do NOT let anyone see me right now!* I made sure he got to his car okay. He was definitely struggling, but not to the point where I thought he needed urgent care of anything! I asked him if he was alright to drive, did he want me to follow him home? He huffed and puffed out, "No way I'm fine, I just need to get my inhaler!" He hopped in his car and off he screeched. I was really confused and taken back by the whole thing. I thought to myself, *what is going ON right now, this is the most absurd night and why is there always a CRAZY STORY?* Now I have to go find my friends because it was still light out and tell them my pizza night was cut short because my, maybe date, had an allergy attack under the tree and almost stopped breathing!

I walked to my car and called Gwen. She was on her date and picked up, "Helloooooooo." I said, "Where are you, my date had an asthma attack, in my face and almost died!" She screeched, "WHAT! Get down here, a few of his friends showed up, we are at Temple Grille." Then she hung up on me. Luckily, Temple Grille was a fun bar and right down the street from where I was, so I sped on over to Temple Grille and I definitely needed a DRINK!

I walk in and scan the crowd. I see Gwen, her date, whose name I forgot and two guys. I pulled myself together and sashayed on over, as if I was cool. These boys had no idea what a loser I just was sweating in the pizza place and then running my asthmatic date to the car! "Helloooooo", I said back to Gwen. "Hey girl! Jim, this is Ella, my roommate, Ella this is my friend Jim and this is Dan and Joe." "Hi everyone, nice to meet you!" I waved. Then I went right to the bar and got a drink. I walked right back up to Gwen, who seemed happy to see me because she was the only girl. I immediately started to tell her the story and we were just laughing. Then she made me tell the three guys what happened. Of course, they were laughing and chuckling, "Poor dude, he's so embarrassed right now, you are not getting a call back." Nice, thanks! *My date cannot breathe under a tree and I DO NOT GET A CALL BACK? But I did not want a call back, okay whatever, I am buzzed*, I thought. So, Dan, one of the two guys accompanying Gwen and Jim was overly paying attention to me. He was so funny, what a great personality! Gwen and I were talking about nonsense, like our cable and how we still need to put a TV in the spare room, blah blah. Dan volunteers to come over in the morning and hook our cable up in the spare room. We were so excited, screeching, "You can do that! Okay awesome!" The night turned into shot fest, dancing in our corner and taking on a few stragglers that we made friends with and SWORE we would keep in touch.

On our way out, we were trying to figure out who had what car, who was driving, and where were we going next. Gwen said, "Well why don't you guys come back to our house and Dan, you can drive Ella's car because you are fine." Okay, so Dan and Joe came with me, to my car, and I handed Dan the keys. Joe hopped in the back seat and we drove home blasting eighties tunes, courtesy of my CDs.

When we walked in, music was already playing, and Gwen was mixing us all some drinks. The after-hours party at the beach house commenced! Nothing over the top exciting was going on. Music was playing, the television was going, and Dan insisted on cooking us eggs! Gwen kept looking at me like Dan was a keeper. She was whispering, "See, he is attentive to you and nice and doing stuff for you, I think he is a keeper." I smiled like she just gave me permission to go in for the kill. I walked into the kitchen and was trying to help him cook. He was telling me what ingredient he needed, and I was just handing it to him from the refrigerator or cupboard. Salt, pepper, butter etc.

This man put out a spread. He had eggs for us, toast and made all of our plates. Then, as I was about to Zamboni my fork across my plate, he squeezed out some ketchup for me. When I looked up at him to say thanks, he bent down and kissed me. This did not seem to alarm anyone; therefore, it did not alarm me. When he sat next to me, I pushed my chair closer to him, grabbed his chin and pulled his face over to me for more kissing.

We kissed and kissed and kissed and danced in the middle of the living room and kissed and kissed ALL over the beach house. I kept saying, "Are you coming back tomorrow to do the cable?" He kept saying "Yea what time?" Gwen stood up from the kitchen table and said "Dan, write your number down on this pad so we can call you tomorrow and make sure you are coming." He grabbed the pad, wrote his name and cell phone down and put the pad down next to our phone. After a bit more banter and some songs played, I felt myself getting tired. I did not feel these boys should drive home. I said, "Guys do not drive home, you need to stay here, and there is plenty of room." Gwen agreed and so did Jim. Gwen and I had no intention of taking anyone back to our bedrooms, but we definitely did not want them to drive. Joe, the outcast, hopped on our couch, Gwen and Jim were still up and I wanted to go to bed. Dan said, "I am going to my car for a minute, be right back." I said, "You can come back in my room if you want but

TO SLEEP!" I thought that was funny and to the point. I went to my bed, hopped in and turned on the television. The second I turned the television on, I realized I was more drunk than I thought. I found the movie Sixteen Candles on some random channel and thought that was a superb selection. I was waiting, what seemed like a very short time, but I must have fallen asleep. What felt like thirty-five seconds was really five hours later! I awoke to the time of eight o'clock in the morning! I was fully clothed and unscathed, television still on and no Dan next to me. I walked into our living room and found it to be vacant, with the music still playing.

I looked down the hall and saw Gwen's door shut. I walked very quietly up to her door and opened it slowly. Gwen was sound asleep in her bed, but no Jim. *Okay, what is going on? No biggie, everyone must have left,* I thought. I was not too pleased with myself because I must have fallen asleep before Dan got back from his car. I had the typical day after jitters, trying to remember what I said, what I did, was I a fool? Then, I remembered all the way back to Dave. *Whoa! What a full night!* I texted Gwen, "Get up now!" and started cleaning the kitchen. I was still trying to piece together exactly what the last thing I said to Dan was and when I fell asleep. I had that nervous stomach that I did something wrong or was he mad that I fell asleep. All the typical feelings a loser, single girl would feel the morning after any crazy Saturday night. Then I remembered, Dan was coming over to do our cable. Yah Fucking hoo! I was good. He was going to come over, we were going to laugh about last night and who knows what else. I really liked him. I turned around with a smirk on my face to get his number from the pad and the pad was not there. *Hmmm,* I thought. I completely recalled him putting his name and number on the pad, placed next to the phone and I was going to call him to tell him what time to come over today. I spun to my left, turned back around, and in the midst of almost vomiting, realized the pad was nowhere to be found.

I went down the hall, to my bedroom, figuring I took the pad with me in the room. No pad ANYWHERE! Where is the Fucking pad???? Before I freaked out, I figured the pad was somewhere! I cleaned the entire kitchen, made coffee, put on television in the living room and waited for Gwen to get up. By the time ten thirty struck, I was no longer hazy from the alcohol and Gwen's door swings open. Best noise I heard all week! The sound of Gwen's door opening. I bolted down the hall, to find her already making her bed. She seemed fine too, no crazy hang over. She said, "Where is everyone?" I said, "I was waiting to ask you the same thing." She said, "I went to bed and they were all watching a movie." I said, "Well they must have left really early." I was not worried because Dan was coming over today, and he still knew where we lived, even though I did not have his number at the moment, because the pad was missing.

Gwen and I walked back to the kitchen for yet another cup of coffee, another pot made for Gwen and I told her I could not find the pad. She said, very casually, "It's over there by the phone. I said "Noooooooo it is not right by the phone!" We both started looking again. Our beach house is NOT big, there are not many places to look. We even looked in the trash, inside, outside to the point that we were assuming this pad had legs or wings! I looked at Gwen and said, "Gwen do you think he took his number back, so I would not call him or find him?" I yell, "Because this is what two grown adults DO on a Sunday, waste a beautiful morning, picking up after another Saturday night bar fest and are hunting down a missing pad with a stranger's phone number on it!" I plopped in the chair, ran my fingers through my hair and said, "I'm not looking for the damn pad and I do not want to think about this for one more second!" I was just so done.

Again, my life flashed before my eyes from being married, then to all the countless dates I took out with the trash, which led to all the work I did taking out my own trash in my head, to Killington, to the stolen mannequin hand to sweating at a pizza parlor to the pad stealer and I was DONE! I felt like I had fallen into an abyss and it was just sucking me up and spitting me BACK OUT!

After my fit was over, in my head, I fell silently to the sounds of the television and continued with my Sunday morning ritual. Sheets, towels and whites cycled through the laundry room. Gwen was in her room, on the phone for the later part of the morning and I was half relaxing. I went out onto the deck. It was another beautiful spring day. I wanted to just chill and look at the water. I could not help but keep thinking to myself, *my friends are having babies right now, my sisters are in their nice houses next door to each other and dealing with real life. So, what's my life amounting to?*

Gwen came out onto the deck. I loved that *swoosh* when I knew the sliding door was opening and my girlfriend was joining me. Made me happy! She sat down next to me and said, "Funny, I called Jim and he is not answering." I replied, "And we can't schedule our cable install because Dan took his number back with the entire pad!" She just started cackling. I did not find it as funny as she did. I was not mad I was just really disappointed. *Do you REALLY think they left and took the pad, so we never called them again? It makes NO SENSE, what if we run into them again,* I thought. But honestly, nothing ever made any sense with these assholes I have been choosing.

Maybe I was on to something before. My friends, sisters and all the people around me having all these great things happening to them; maybe they just simply picked the right men. Maybe they had more self-worth than me and picked men they knew they deserved. These wonderful men are now sharing wonderful lives with them. I know there are good guys out there. My friends and sisters have them! Bottom line, I was still picking garbage. And as I learned year one of my Software Engineering degree, *garbage in.... garbage out!*

Chapter 12

Well Spring has definitely sprung, and I sprung out my trash with my new revelations of "Garbage In....Garbage Out!" I stopped thinking, talking or looking for men! It is so liberating to just live your life without all this trash swirling around in your mental space. I just love working on my family and friend relationships. Since I was in Killington, every Sunday this winter, I missed Sunday macaroni with my entire family. Even Liza's family was included in Sunday macaroni. This tradition started with my Italian family long before I was even born. My father must have his "Ronis" even if it is ninety degrees outside. There are usually, roughly, twenty people for Sunday dinner, which includes my parents, sisters and their families and some of their kid's friends and Liza and her family. There are at least five different meals to choose from, along with the macaroni, and everyone talks over each other. I forgot how special Sundays were.

On this particular Spring Sunday everyone was in a good mood. My two older sisters do not really question me or care what I am doing because they are really involved with their own lives. They usually love just sitting down with me and Liza and live through us and want to hear our funny stories. My father was still extremely disgusted with Liza and I about the mannequin hand and Liza's Mom and my Mom just stay in the kitchen to make sure everyone is fed!

Dessert and *coffee 'an*, comes out. As we engage in the last course, the questions start firing at me from my sister, Donna. She turns to Liza and me, "So are you guys talking to anyone, dating, what's going on? You guys are never around." I was hurt, I really wanted to be around, but I really hated staying around everyone, their husbands and their kids, it really depressed me! I said, "It's not that we are not around, do not take it personally, it is just that we are trying to find single things to do, everyone is always a couple and I do not really like going out with all couples." She got very upset! Donna said, "Ok ya know what, that is ridiculous! So, you are going to hang around BARS, instead of being with us and waste your time with strangers, that makes no sense!" She shook her head, looked away and Liza and I stared at each other. She was right! She was so right! I could not even argue with her.

The rest of Sunday dinner was fun, and I made a little pact in my own head to really work on my connection with my sisters and my friends. The ones with kids, without kids, with husbands, without husbands, these people were my rock through really hard times and deserve my love, loyalty and attention. Instead, I am giving it to these stupid men I do not even know!

I kissed everyone goodbye and made a plan to throw out dates for dinner with my sisters and more of my friends, that I have not seen all winter. As I was driving home, I realized the sun was still out after dinner which was so nice! When I pulled up to my driveway, there was this beautiful pink haze in the blue sky with the sun setting in the water. Absolutely breathtaking! So breathtaking that it actually made me upset. No matter what stupid little pacts I have in my head, I was sad that I did not have anyone to share this beautiful sunset with.

But wait, oh yes, I did have someone to share the sunset with! Gwen was sitting on the deck with a glass of wine! I walked in quick to drop my bag and went right out onto the patio. "Hey girl", she said with a huge smile on her face. I said, "What's going on?" I plopped myself down in the patio chair and we just started talking about Sunday dinner. I told her what my Sister said, and she agreed. I was calm and happy about what I learned today and just stared out at the water. Then Gwen said, "It's your birthday soon! What do you want to do?" *Oh Frig!* I thought, *yes, it is!*

I just politely said, "I don't care! It falls on Memorial Day Weekend, so we have a full weekend of Birthday fun! Let's just pick one of the nights, and a place and just tell everyone to meet there. I know my sisters will come and a bunch of my friends, and Liza, Robyn and Jaime will definitely be there. Gwen said, "Perfect!" I got up from my chair and went inside. Got myself all ready for Monday again, laundry, dusting, shower and regrouping!

This Monday was interesting. Scott came to my desk, early, to shoot the Shit. We made it out of our Killington lease, unscathed, and managed to have a few laughs about the window, now that it was all behind us. He went back to his desk which was down the hall and I just continued on with my tasks and boring reports. At the end of the day, I got a call from Gwen. She wanted to meet out for dinner. I was all about it because I did not feel like cooking. I called Gwen from the car and we decided it was a good idea to go to Tommy Sullivan's Irish Pub for some appetizers. I walked into Monday night happy hour, half price wings and two-dollar beers. Nice for a Monday!

Gwen and I got a table for two and released all our Monday blues into the air with two great big sighs at the same time! She started in on her day. She has two ladies at work who are fighting, and I proceeded to tell her that I was coding all day long and literally, did not speak for seven hours. These two gentlemen sit next to us at another table for two. We smiled, they smiled, and we carried on with our discussions. The subject of dating came up and I asked Gwen if she ever talked to that guy she went on a date with back in the winter. I cannot keep her dates straight. We all know what happened with Jim, he was never heard from again and his friend, the pad stealer also went missing. But she had a few other dates and I felt bad not asking her if anything developed. Gwen is good though, she really just "moves on."

She mentioned that the guy was okay, but no sparks, and he never called her for a second date, and that was fine with her. As she is talking about how guys need to get over themselves and stop thinking they can get young girls when they are fat and bald, I noticed the men next to us sort of eavesdropping and smirking. Then I engaged in Gwen's comments, offering up the fact that not only do they think they can still get young girls, but they think they are geniuses and yet are complete idiots. Well, these men next us could not resist but to jump into our conversation.

"Now hold on a minute," the cuter of the two guys sitting on the same side of me said, as he was holding his pint of IPA. "You two sound like those typical man-haters, what did the last guy to do you that left you with that last assumption?" I replied, as I was holding my heart, "It's not that anyone did anything to me, I just am completely exhausted by dating and I'm just taking a break. Please don't ask me to share anymore or you will be sprinting out of here like Roadrunner!" He started laughing and pointed to his friend, "This is Mike and I'm Ray." I reciprocated with a nod over to Gwen, "This is Gwen and I'm Ella." Ray said, "Ella, what nationality is that?" I said, "Seriously, I'm Italian." Ray replied kind of snotty, "Ok well you have such dark features, I almost thought you were Lebanese." "LEBANESE!", I screamed. Not that there is anything wrong with that, but what an idiot!

The four of us, then engaged in some quick-witted banter about dating, online dating and trying to meet people after divorce. I did not share much with them, other than the fact that I was divorced with no kids and Gwen had never been married and was really not looking to get married, either. These men shared that they were both divorced and seemed harmless, funny and smart. It was so nice to talk to normal guys. They were both very mature and were both accountants. Boring, yes, but so was engineering and the last guy I spent time with was a pill popping, boozing bartender, so I had no business judging.

When our food was served, each table sort of reverted back into private conversation. Gwen and I were talking about my birthday and Ray leaned in, "It's your birthday, how old?" I said, "No not today, but soon, and I'm not telling you how old I am!" He let out a cocky, toss head back chuckle and said "Well, must be nice to be in your twenties still." I was sooooooooo smitten, I clenched my chest and replied ecstatically, "Okay you are my new best friend because I am NOT in my twenties." *Heeee heeeee, giggle giggle*, here I go acting like a complete ASS again. Gwen was giggling and opened her eyes really WIDE. I whispered across the table, "What?". She said, under her breath, "I like him. Do not leave without his number." I said, "For you?" She said, "No, YOU, idiot!" Then she kicked me under the table. I said, "Oh no, no way!" Yea right, within the next ten minutes, the men picked up our tab, Ray and I had each other's number and we had a date for drinks this coming Friday night.

We headed on over to our cars and Gwen said, "I gotta hand it to you, you do always get dates and guys are always interested in you." I said, "Yes but that does not mean I have to act on every single one! I'm flattered, but I am the one who can pass on some of these assholes." We both hopped in our

138

cars and drove home. By the time I got home, Ray had already texted-

Great meeting you, Ella. See you Friday

I wrote-

Same here, looking forward to it

When we arrived back at the house, I barreled in the door and turned behind to Gwen saying, "Who is this man? I don't even know his last name?" She said, "Just get to know each other during the week, who cares." Well, throughout the week, I ended up getting his last name, where he lived, where he worked, and we exchanged some funny chit chat back and forth. I felt much more comfortable for Friday night.

As Friday morning approached, I decided to just go to work, not think about this "meeting" I had with Ray and just be casual. I, impatiently, made it through the morning, Ray texted-

TGIF

I replied-

TGIF!!!

Ray-

What time is good for you tonight?

Me-

Anytime, I get home around 6

Now, I am pondering whether or not we are eating dinner because he said "meet for drinks" but I said 6 o'clock, so this could be "Friday happy hour meet for drinks," but I was not sure. Ray replied-

Meet me at 6, Tommy's, same as last time

I replied-

Perfect

It appeared to me to be a "meet and greet" for drinks, happy hour, no dinner and no dressing up like I'm going to dinner and the theatre. I snuck out a bit early and got myself home just in time to freshen up and run back out of the house.

I was driving very slowly. I wanted to be five minutes late, but I was still so early. I looked so stupidly anxious if I showed up first, perched on a bar stool, waiting for some man I hardly knew. I found myself at Tommy Sullivan's twelve minutes, too early. I proceeded to drive back down the street, waste gas, like a fool, and then I pulled into a funeral home parking lot to check my face, again. My stomach was in a full pit! I hated walking in places by myself, but I just had to take that out with the trash. People go to restaurants alone all the time! I have to be confident enough to be able to BE ALONE, walk in places ALONE and maybe even some day, live ALONE.

I pulled out slowly and headed down the street, back in the direction of Tommy Sullivan's. It was still light out on this nice Spring Friday evening. I look up at the outside deck as I am walking into the main entrance. I see Ray outside, sitting at a table. It was not very warm out but was nice to sit outside and get some fresh air. I walked over to the table with a very nice, confident, pretty smile. He stood up, kissed me on the cheek and we both sat down.

We both were smiling and staring at each other with a little bit of exhaustion in our faces from a typical work week. He asked what I wanted to drink. I ordered a Bud Light. I probably should learn to drink a more sophisticated drink, but Bud Light was safe on no dinner! He starts the conversation, "So Ella...", then grabs my hand across the table. It was very nice, any girls dream, but I was stretching my eyeballs from left to right sweeping the happy hour population on the deck hoping NO ONE would see me. I was sort of fake smiling and replied, "Yes, how was your week?" He let go of my hand and sat way back, away from me. He was actually pretty handsome. I would say he was over six feet, light brown hair and nice fair skin. His hair was styled very nicely and had a really nice business casual outfit on from work. The only thing I hate, is when men cross their legs and he was in a full cross, clenching his knee with both hands. He proceeded to talk about the mundane life of an accountant. I then proceeded to talk about my snore of a life as an engineer. This date was definitely not material for a juicy reality show. At least not yet!

Drinks were flowing, we ordered a few appetizers and I was actually having a very good time. I realized, this man is just "normal." It was refreshing to have a normal, mature, professional guy that was so different from the Killington guys, who were out to booze and play all weekend long on the mountain. Ray ended up telling me all about his job, travel and just sort of casually grazed over the fact that he was "going through a divorce." I did not want to ask questions, nor did I want to bash the exes and tell war stories, so I just replied, "Been there, it sucks doesn't it?" He said, "Oh yes, I would not wish it on my worst enemy!" And I appreciated that, he did not wife bash or appear scorned like divorcees I previously dated. He was mature! It was dark and cold now! As I was putting on my jacket, I said, "Don't worry I am not leaving, I'm just freezing." He looked around the deck and said, "We should probably go in, it still gets cold when the sun goes down." I replied, "Oh yes we are not there yet with summer evenings, still cold all spring. My birthday always falls on Memorial Day Weekend and every time I plan something outdoors, I forget it is still cold out!" He then suavely inquired, "Will I be invited to this year's birthday bash?"

Well, now there you go! My birthday was weeks away, so I pulled the ole over analyzation and thought, o*h this man wants to date me, he is talking "long term."* I flirtingly said, "Ummm if you play your cards right!" Then, I walked into the bar in front of him with a big smile on my face. We found some real estate at the bar and ordered two more drinks. We were telling funny stories about growing up and what sitcoms we both liked to watch as a kid. It was mindless drivel, but it broke the ice and I felt very comfortable with him. He did not even run when I told him I still get teary eyed when I hear the "Eight Is Enough" theme song, because it reminds me of my childhood. When, in reality, I do not frequently hear the "Eight Is Enough" theme song. I was just talking nonsense! There was not a moment of silence between our conversations. I found myself standing up, securing myself in between his knees. He was rubbing my arm and I was feeling a lot of chemistry for the first time in a while!

As we threw back our final drink, he said, "Is it too late for you to come back to my house to hang out for a bit?" I got really nervous. I thought to myself, is this the longest happy hour turned one-night stand in the history of my life or is he having that much fun with me that he really just wanted to hang out more and get to know me? I tossed all caution to the wind, shrugged my shoulders and said, "Sure, it's not too late, it's only nine o'clock!" His whole face lit up, he leaned in and gave me the sweetest, softest kiss on the lips. My heart was pounding. *I rrreallly liked this guy.* I turn towards the exit, looking around, as we pass through the crowd thinking I struck gold. We held hands in the parking lot and he walked me to my car first and said, "Wait here until I pull around, then you can follow me." I looked up at him with dreamy eyes and he leaned in and kissed me again, before he shut the car door.

OH MY GOD! I am dizzy with excitement and waiting eagerly with my reverse lights already on! He pulls around in a tremendous Lexus and I was just hooked on his looks, his maturity and his charm. I follow him into the shoreline area of our town and getting happier and happier as we approach the finer streets of the waterfront neighborhood. I am BLASTING Mariah Carey for some reason which is a total embarrassment, but I did not even care. I did not even know what planet I was on, I was so high on life right now.

We pull onto this lavish, gorgeous cobblestone path and let our tires roll very slowly down the long driveway to his exquisite home. It was a very grand, very modern waterfront home, coated in a cottony, taupe stucco, with sharp frames and white contemporary trim. The second I stepped out of the car, I immediately fussed to Ray over how beautiful this home was. He was very humble and appreciative of my compliments. He was staring at the front door with a blank, disturbed look on his face. I slowly leaned in from the back of him and asked, "Is everything OK?" He hesitated to turn and answer me. Then he said, "Yes, I just don't remember leaving these lights on in the foyer, for a second I thought someone might be here." I said, "Oh who?" He replied, "Just thought for a minute my ex-wife was here that's all." My stomach plunged to my toes, I actually, completely forgot he was going through a divorce because my head was stuck in a cloud from the first barstool kiss!

He was very gracious, smiled and put his hand on my back to lead me to the front porch. He was making small talk asking if I wanted another drink, as he was opening the front door. I had never been in this outstanding home before, but as I walked into the foyer, I felt an energy and a presence of chaos for some reason. Either it was my intuition or crazy energy lingering through the stairways, but something felt *off.*

The house was a beautiful open floor plan with floor to ceiling windows and sliders looking out onto the beautiful ocean. As it was night time, the moon, the stars and the glisten of the water were like a piece of art. I walked directly over to the slider to see the view and mask my slight feeling of awkwardness, when I hear a shriek from Ray, "WHAT THE FUUUUCK!" I turn around, in a panic and saw that there were piles and piles of paper torn and shredded in the middle of his living room. I looked up from the floor and took in the sight of his beautiful shelving, which encased a large flat screen TV. These bookcases were completely mangled. I jerked my focus to the right and noticed that side was empty, then the other side had book covers toppled and piled on the shelves, half hanging off onto the floor. I walked over to the book covers and realized all the pages were missing. As I looked over at Ray, he bent down at the pile of paper and said, "She ripped all of the pages out of all my books!" I screeched, "WHO?" He said, "MY EX-WIFE!"

My entire body, along with my expression froze. I did not know whether to run, comfort him or hide in a closet, in case she was still in the house! I stuttered, "Oh my.... oh, I'm so sorry, what happened, why?" He said they had been fighting all day and she wanted to come back home. I sarcastically replied, "Come back home?" He said, yes well, we have only been separated for a few weeks and she does not really want this, it has been a nightmare. I said, "Why is SHE not in the home?" He said, "It's a long story, she's crazy." *She's crazy? A few weeks?* I wanted to die!

The room was silent, and my buzz was instantly killed. I just bent down and started picking up the shredded pages of his collection of classics. Pages of *Pride and Prejudice*, pieces of *The Catcher In The Rye* and strips of *Moby Dick* were spattered about, all over this poor bastard's coffee table and oriental rug. As I am picking up the empty book cover bindings behind me, I thought of the girls in my head and how I was going to tell them about this. I started laughing on the inside and was trying desperately not to chuckle or snort, but I was nervous and silly. I said, "I'm sorry I don't mean to overstep my bounds here, but why is she doing this?" He defeatedly replied, "Because I told her it is definitely over, and she said she was going to spend every day making my life a living hell." I said, "Well, I've been through this before and it really sucks for the person who doesn't want the divorce, but you really need to be careful here, this looks disturbing!"

Honestly, this is the last bit of drama I need or feel like dealing with right now! I have been divorced for a while, I had a ridiculous ride so far and I am PISSED that this perfect "meet and greet" had turned into a fiasco! We stood up and I said, "Maybe I should go." He grabbed both my hands and said, "No please stay, please have a drink with me, I'm so sorry you had to see this, but don't leave me." And of course, I turned to jelly and put my rescue cape on and had to stay with this poor man. I know in my head that a normal woman would probably bow out gracefully and screech down the street when she got out of the driveway but noooooooooo, not me! So, he holds my hand and leads me into the kitchen, and screeches again, "What the FUCK!" My instant reaction was, "What is going ON RIGHT NOW?" As I yelled that very statement, he rushed over to the sink. In the sink was every single wine and champagne glass that they owned, with the stems cracked off. There was a note that stated, "Have fun having whores over for a glass of wine, Asshole!"

I am completely dying, shaking and laughing inside, all at the same time. I was a bit scared too. I yelled, "Is she in this house right now!" My whole life flashed before my eyes, AGAIN, and all I can think of is this crazy lady, attacking me or slicing me up with the stem of one of the glasses, so I FREAKED OUT! "Ray, you need to call the cops right now!" He said, "No, I don't want to do that, she's just blowing off some steam." *Steam?* I'm pretty sure this behavior is more than "blowing off steam!"

Ray started looking around, peering around corners on the first floor of this home, and I was following close behind. I did not want to leave his side, in case I had to hide behind him. I was afraid of the ex-wife jumping out of a closet with a hatchet. He grabbed my hand, again, and led me up the stairs. I really did want to help this guy but I just could NOT believe this was actually happening. Next time I need to do some research when someone says, "I'm going through a divorce."

We approach the top of the stairs. It appeared to be a master suite with more sliders and windows overlooking the gorgeous sound. He screeched, "I KNEW IT!" I gasped for air, clenched my chest and winced, "Oh noooo!" There was a pile of clothing near the closet door. It appeared to be a mountain of men's clothing on the hardwood floor, with a miniature version of the same pile right next to it. We both slowly walked over to the scene and started slowly picking up each article of clothing that had every single sleeve ripped off the and tossed to the side! This man had Vineyard Vine casual, Versace and Bottega Veneta suits and a variety of luxury brands that would make Trump's closet look like Walmart! All pieces of clothing had every sleeve sliced off at the shoulder seam. It was the creepiest and most chilling scene, yet all I could do was burst out laughing. I got so scared and so nervous, I just could not get rid of this nervous laugh. I put my hand on his arm and said, "I am so sorry I do NOT think this is funny, I'm just really nervous right now." He gave me a dirty look and said, "I think you better go." I half giggled, "Yes." My eyes were tearing going down the flight of stairs because I was laughing inside so HARD. I could hear his footsteps following me down the staircase. He did feel horribly embarrassed and I did feel bad for the dude. I turned and said, "Ray you need to wait a little bit before you bring girls back to your house." I gave him a sad face and he said, "I guess I didn't think it through." I gave him a huge hug and wished him luck.

I walked to the car with my head down. I was so puzzled. I could not believe this actually happened. I actually drove home with no music on and was completely silent. It was a little after ten o'clock. As I approached my house, I saw Gwen was home, she did not even start her night yet. I walked in and plopped myself down in the chair, I looked exhausted and harried! Gwen took one look at me and said in disgust "What is the matter NOW?" I looked up at her with long puppy dog eyes, then burst into an exhausted laughter and told her the entire story. We were laughing, and she had a series of interrupted questions because she was so confused. Then Gwen had the audacity to say, "Well are you going to see him again?" I said, "Not without his docket number and a restraining order for his ex!" I stood up and dragged my ass to my bedroom and just went to bed. The end!

The next morning, I cleaned my whole room, looked out onto the ocean to welcome another beautiful Saturday morning and for the first time in a while, I was just looking forward to spending Saturday night home, by myself!

Chapter 13

This particular Saturday was very productive. I had a major epiphany when I woke up at seven o'clock in the morning. I had not been out late, hung over or riddled with guilt over something dumb I had done the night before. I just took Ray out with the morning trash! I took more than Ray out with the trash this morning. As I made my coffee, cleaned up some old clutter in the kitchen from the week's events, and stuffed some garbage in the trash, my epiphany was that I liked being with myself more than being with all these strange men for the sake of dating. The trash was being smooshed down and compacted in this garbage bag with such passion this morning. I just wanted to get rid of everything, including the clutter in my head. This was the first Saturday I was thrilled that I had nothing to do and no date! Why would I want to spend my valuable time with these guys and their garbage, when I work really hard all week. I just deserve a peaceful night! If this means being alone, I know I will have more fun, be able to eat and watch what I want to watch on television. If I stay home, peacefully alone, I know I will not be taking in any of their garbage into MY Saturday night!

After I dumped the trash bag into the big bin in our driveway, I went inside to grab my coffee and proceeded to the back deck to enjoy the beautiful sunlight and the water views. The sound of the waves lapping up against the cement walls of my shoreline patio was so calming. I shut my eyes and had a moment. Then I hear the *shwooooosh* of the sliding glass door. Gwen walked out with her coffee and our Saturday morning talk began. I told her about my epiphany and she said, "Good for you, I love it!" And as she said that, I turned my head with a huge smile. We both sipped our coffees and decided to try to lay in the sun with some magazines and simply chill out on this first very warm Spring Saturday.

We went inside to put our shorts and tank tops on and rushed right back out with some magazines and our phones. It was the first sunbath of Spring, when you will not put a bathing suit on and sit up with your legs up on a different chair. It just was not officially summer yet, so we could not commit to full lounge chairs, suits and oil. But the sun sure did feel fabulous!

My phone rang, it was Robyn, "Hey girlfriend!" I very happily greeted her, "Good morning sister, how was your week?" She proceeded to tell me all about her work week and blah blah blah and said, "How was your date?" I just sunk in my chair and moaned, "Oh girrrrl not so good!" I proceeded to tell her the entire story and she was laughing, as usual, and then got very serious and said, "El, I hope she doesn't know about you!" *Yeah that would suck*, I thought. That is all I friggin need is some crazy wife after me, I'm too tired for this Shit!

Next call, "Hi Mom!", "Hi, my sweetheart!", she replied. She then proceeded to talk to me about my sister's cold, how many chicken cutlets she fried and made thirty meatballs for dinner on Sunday. Then literally hung up in my face. I do not think I actually spoke. I just hung up the phone. That is usually how we all communicate in my family.

As my eyes were closed, soaking in the sun, Gwen yelled, "Hey guys!" I opened my eyes and saw she was waving over at Giovanni and Pajama Pants Paul. They came out onto Giovanni's deck with coffee. It was not noon yet, but had to be around eleven o'clock in the morning, at this point. It looked to me like Paul had slept over. I smirked and said, "Late night boys!" And just as I was about to stand up and walk over to the railing of my deck, *Shwooooosh*, their slider opened and out walked two bombshell girls with their "night" clothes on. They were shielding the blinding sun with the palms of their hands and sat down. Now I am dying!

Not one of the four of them were talking to each other. Gwen and I are whispering and trying very hard to mock them, then gave up because they were both skinny and gorgeous! I heard a little small talk and then opened one eye to try to sneak a peak of the guys, walking them to the front, where their car was parked. It was a dumb VW Bug, very cutesy of course!

Paul walks up onto our deck and sits at the patio table. "What's shaking ladies?" I sing songy sang back, "Nothiiiiiiiing." And then I looked over to him with a big sarcastic smile. I wanted him to tell us ALL about their one-night stands, but he was not forth coming with information. He did not offer, so I did not ask. He asked, "What are you guys up to today?" I very happily said, "Nothing, absolutely nothing and I cannot wait to stay home tonight with take-out and a good Lifetime Television for Women movie!" He shrugged away from me like I was some crazy vixen, "Alrighty then, crazy girl!" I just laughed. Giovanni now graced us with his presence and sat in the chair next to Gwen. We were all just chatting about our week and found ourselves ready for lunch. Gwen decided that we should all have lunch together and brought out some hot dogs to grill and chips. However, we had nothing but tap water or flat soda, so Giovanni grabbed some beers and water bottles from his house. Paul lit up our grill and a nice impromptu lunch was served oceanside.

I was trying to keep the conversation going, not that it was awkwardly silent, but just enjoying the company. "I cannot believe it is my birthday in a few weeks!" Paul slammed his hand on the table, "Birthday keg!" I looked at him funny, "Birthday keg?" I snarked. I wanted to go out and do something fun, not have a "birthday keg" like I was in college! Then Gwen said, "Let's keep it low key and go out for a nice dinner and drinks and if anyone wants to join us they can." Sounded perfect to me. PJ Paul responded, "I'm in, let us know." I said, "Gwen, can we do my actual birthday because it falls on the Sunday of Memorial Day weekend and we do not have to work the next day?" She replied, "Perfect!"

As the day wrapped up, I felt a bit tired from the sun and was very excited to spend my Saturday night alone! Gwen wanted to stay in too. This was nice! We voluntarily wanted to stay in and had no problem being alone with ourselves on a Saturday night. What a concept? We were even too lazy to make a different dinner, so we put more hot dogs on the grill! It was a typical single girl scenario! We had minimal groceries, did not have to worry about feeding a husband or a child and did not have to hear any of the complaining from anyone else in the house. My epiphany just got a little bit deeper. I am finally realizing my life is actually kind of awesome!

Chapter 14

A few weeks went by, one running into the next. A lot of working and a lot of "nothing" on the social life front. I talk to my friends and family every single day but there was nothing pressing going on until this weekend coming up, my birthday! It was Thursday of Memorial Day weekend. Gwen and I decided to come home from work and get all of our laundry, cleaning and all other chores done so that we can start Friday off with a bang! I was collecting the small trash bags in our bedrooms and bathroom and consolidating all the garbage into one large bag. I do not know why I gravitate towards the trash when after all these years, I still really hate it! Maybe I do it with justification that I am taking out my "trash" and it makes me feel cleaner or clearer, I do not know! I just send the garbage out every time I take it in! That seems to be happening with the men I have been dating too.

I have not had a date since the Ray debacle. I have been out over the past few weeks and socialized, but nothing worth getting excited over. I did have one guy ask for my number at a work happy hour. He said he was getting divorced. I looked at him in complete disgust and said, "Please don't talk to me until you can produce a docket number!" He looked at me like I was psycho, yet I was just experiencing post-traumatic stress from Ray telling me he was "getting divorced."

I took the trash outside and finished folding my laundry, as Gwen was vacuuming, there was a knock at the door. It was Paul. He walked in with a clear cellophane package of white roses! My eyes lit up and he walked over to me and said, "For the birthday girl!" I fussed so much! I kept saying, "Oh how sweet, it is not my birthday until Sunday!" He insisted on giving them to me now and said he was going to Rhode Island in the morning but would be back for my birthday. I gave him a huge hug good bye and a very nice innocent, friendly kiss on the lips, but it was a bit longer than usual. I walked him to the door and closed it behind him. I turned to Gwen with a very appreciative look and just said, "So nice!"

Gwen was so excited and said, "Ella, I think he does really like you." I shrugged my shoulders and started to open the cellophane, so we could get these roses in water. The packaged flowers were very condensed into this cellophane, it was weird. When I pulled apart the squished roses, out from the inside appeared rotten, brown, dead, white roses. I said under my breath, "What the Fuck. Oh my God, GWEN!" She walked over to the kitchen table and said with a very snotty tone, "Oh my God, they are DEAD!"

I defeatedly put the rose I was holding in my hand back in the sad, wilted pile and just started laughing and shaking my head, again! As always, the laughter starts because I just cannot FUCKING believe the crazy things that go on in my life. WHY did this guy even bother buying me roses if he needed to buy cheap, disgusting, gas station roses? This package looked like it was sitting in one of those buckets at the register of a gas station convenience store! And it probably was there for a while because the roses were brown and rotting!

Gwen was getting so silly, she kept taking them out of the cellophane and said, "We have to put these out on display." Now this just became entertainment for us! I said, "Go ahead, put them in a vase and keep them out to remind me of how special I am that I got rotted roses for my birthday!" Gwen replied, "Now that is not nice, he probably didn't have the money to buy you good roses, it was the thought that counted." I squawked back, "Buy NO roses! If you can't afford roses, buy NO ROSES, buy NOTHING, we are not even dating!" Then I just got silly and I went in my bedroom and grabbed my camera. I started taking pictures because I needed the documentation to look back on in the future, when hopefully life will be better and include fresh roses! I went into my bedroom and got myself ready for bed. I could not wait for this birthday weekend to start. I turned the television on but was not really watching. I was thinking. I was trying to find a reason to care about the rotted roses. I was trying to have a pity party and could not gather a good enough one that even I wanted to attend. Usually, I kick off the pity party with "SURPRISE.! Why me??" Now I realize the answer. Not everyone in my life needs to be "the man." Paul should just be some sweet guy, who has been an old friend, who tried really nicely, out of the kindness of his heart, to think of another friend on her birthday. Why am I trying to feel sorry for myself over the dead roses? These roses were not from my husband of twenty years! They were just gas station roses! Why do I always have to build up every man to be "the one," like a stupid fairytale? This ridiculous line of thinking, that I have concocted in my head, is garbage and that is why I'm always taking out my trash. Garbage in IS garbage OUT!

As I was relaxing, in bed, I wanted to do a mental timeline of my life, from my childhood, where things were normal, stable and wonderful. I let some memories flash before my eyes, as I stared at the ceiling. I could not stop smiling! I had a great childhood! Then I progressed to the teenage years and college, which were the absolute greatest times of my life! And then, I thought about Chuck, my husband. The good part of our life. It was wonderful, he was a great guy, just had an addiction that came between us and our marriage ended in turmoil! From then on, I cannot even remember anything, except trying so desperately to fill that void, that I forgot who I am and how GREAT my life is!

The more time has gone on in this past month, the more I realize how much I really love myself! I am loving myself too much to waste time on all this hard work, trying to find a man who is not worth a few hours of my time on a Saturday night! I want things to be peaceful and happen organically, when I least expect it. And if it does not, it is ok, because my life is kind of great and I am kind of fabulous! Just as I started to relax into the appendix to my original epiphany, Gwen knocked on my door. She had her hair in a towel, as she had just finished showering. She said, very annoyed, "We forgot to take the garbage down to the curb, it's Thursday!" I was completely fine and eager to help. I smiled cheerfully and said, "No worries, I got it!!"

I perked up, out of bed. As I casually strolled down the driveway, I knew this week's trash in my head was going OUT! Walking back to the house, I was looking forward to tomorrow, my birthday weekend ahead and every week after that. From then on, I was the one who happily, always took out the trash!

CPSIA information can be obtained
at www.ICGtesting.com
Printed in the USA
LVHW092002221118
597951LV00001B/4/P

9 781644 381847